Queens of the Fae book Twelve

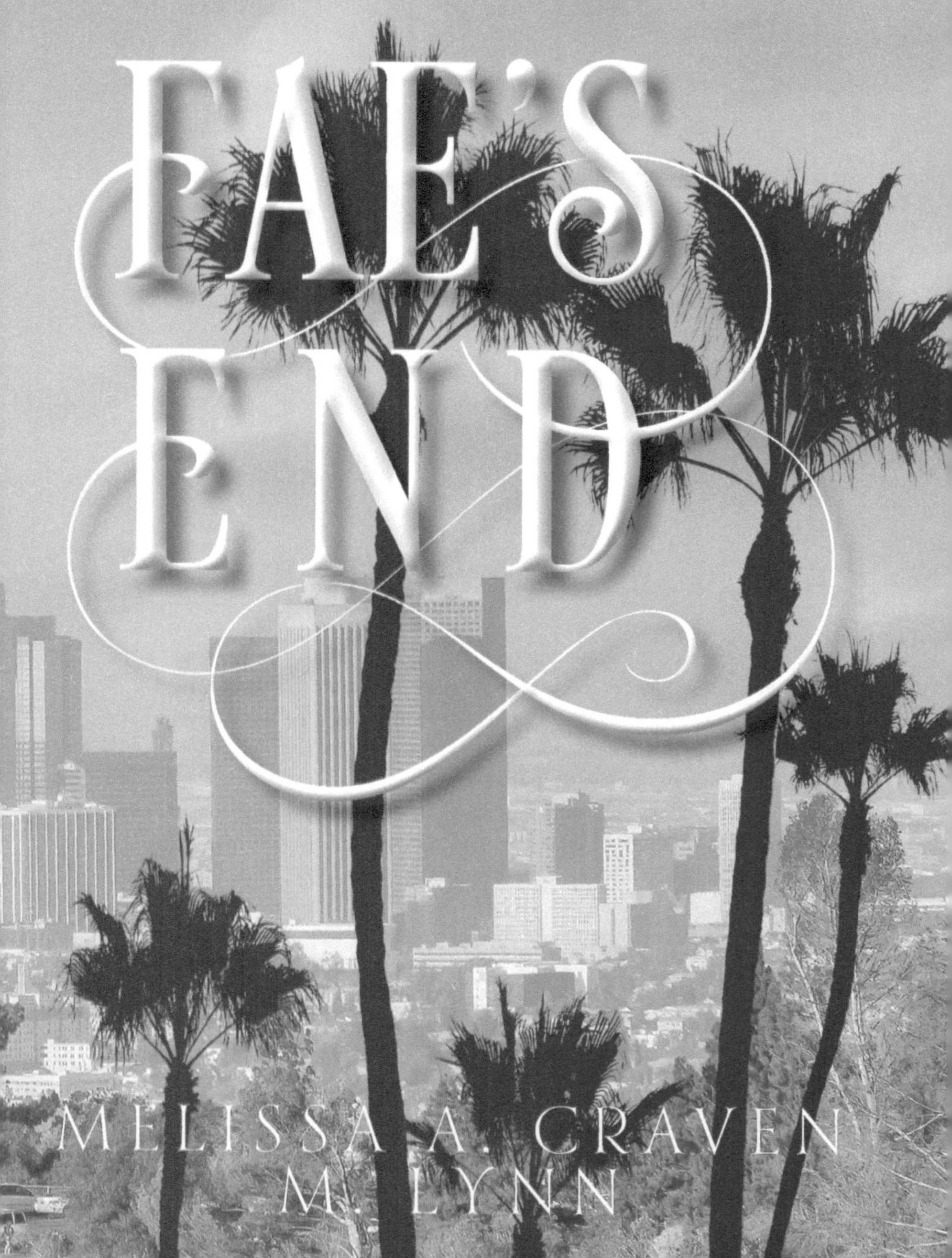
FAE'S
END
MELISSA A. CRAVEN
M. LYNN

Edited by Caitlin Haines
Cover by Maria Spada

Chapter One
GULLIVER

Smoke filled the air as another explosion cracked against the weakening shields over Aghadoon.

"Get down!" Toby ran at Gulliver, smashing into him and sending them both to the cobblestones. The building behind them erupted, raining down rocks and rubble on their heads.

Toby covered him with his body.

Breath wheezed in Gullie's lungs as he stared up at the hole in Aghadoon's shield, a shield of magic that was supposed to be impenetrable. But this wasn't magic. At least, not in the fae sense. The human's technology had proven to be more powerful than even Tia's magic.

"You okay?" Toby yelled in his ear.

But the ringing in Gulliver's own ears drowned out his voice as Toby climbed off him.

"We have to get to cover." Gullie's voice wasn't loud enough, but he couldn't seem to yell, not amidst the chaos of the battle.

Toby yanked him to his feet, and they took off running.

"Gullie, I could use your magic." Griff waved him toward the library.

Gullie stumbled after him. "How?" No one ever needed the defensive powers of the dark fae. Except now, it was still more than what the half-fae had.

They reached the library that held every bit of magic known to fae kind. If they lost this ... well, Gullie wasn't sure if the library could be destroyed, but he didn't want to find out. He'd seen what the burning of a spell did. It no longer existed. They'd destroyed the marriage bonds that way, and now, every other power that existed in their world was at risk.

By bringing Aghadoon to the human realm as a place of refuge, they may have doomed magic itself.

"We have to protect the library." Griff lifted his hands, creating a shield between them. The moon had only barely risen in the sky, so his power would grow, but for now, it had to be enough. "I need you to focus on your magic, Gullie. Like you never have before. There's a chance we could use it to buy us more time."

Gulliver concentrated. Dark Fae magic was like a built-in armor. It was just there. But now he needed to extend that protection as far as he could. He couldn't do it on his own. His power didn't work that way. Griff had to try to pull it from him, using his own magic to turn that of the Dark Fae into something more useful.

An explosion sounded behind him, followed by Xavier screaming orders.

"Everyone down!"

Griff didn't move. "Not us, Gulliver."

"Dad." A tear leaked from his eye as he fought to strengthen Griffin's shield, to hold on to the thread of power feeding into his father. It was like nothing he'd ever felt before. The raw power of his defensive magic seared his chest, flooding his body with a strange energy.

"Hold on, Gullie." Griff shouted over the explosions from the human weapons.

But he didn't know how this worked. "I can't hold it." He grappled with the power he didn't know how to control.

"Yes, you can. You have to."

He gritted his teeth, letting loose a roar as his muscles contracted and Griff pulled the magic from him, somehow boosting his own.

Gullie had been to war before, but this time was different. When the fae battled, they were on mostly even footing. Magic against magic.

The humans had the power to wipe them from the face of their world with weapons they'd never seen. And they wanted that more than anything.

A plane came into view over the village, and Gullie could hear the half-fae leaders shouting to those who'd come to fight, but he couldn't make out what they were saying.

Someone sprinted toward them, and Gullie sensed Brandon's magic the moment he joined forces with Griffin in protecting the library. The three of them were the only ones with any kind of significant power in this village, but the village itself did its best to deflect the raining fire from the violent human weapons.

They'd barely seen any human warriors, but the humans

didn't need to come out to fight when they had what Xavier called bombs and missiles.

"Keep going." Brandon's voice was calm, certain. He gave no indication that he realized he was one of the reasons magic was in danger. If anyone said that to him, he'd most likely respond with the fact that the half-fae of L.A. were also mostly still alive because the village had been there to protect them. *What's more important, Gulliver? Magic or fae?*

He'd always thought they were one and the same. A fae was nothing without the power they were meant to have. But then, he saw Tia lose it and find herself. He witnessed a kingdom where magic was scarce but hope was still alive. If this library burned up right now, their way of life would change, but they'd still have those lives.

Gulliver turned to Brandon as his father's pull on his magic waned. "We need to get everyone into the village."

He'd broken the unspoken rule of the fae once. Those with human blood were not to be taken to their world. But Myles ... Alona ... Sophie. The world hadn't ended because they broke a rule.

"Where are you going?" Griffin yelled.

Gullie looked back over his shoulder. "We're taking them to the fae realm. Prepare the village."

Griff opened his mouth likely to protest, but then seemed to think better of it. Brandon didn't hesitate to run for the village square, where he would work the ancient stones to move the village.

Orla was near the broken pillars at the front gate, shards of rock at her feet. This woman led the fae of L.A. She'd kept them safe until now. Would she agree to a retreat?

"Gullie, get back inside," she yelled, shoving him behind her as another flying death machine circled the village. Lines of half-fae took cover outside the village, aiming their weapons into the sky.

Fire erupted from the back of the machine, and it veered toward the ground. Fae scrambled out of the way, some launching into the air as a crash shook the earth beneath their feet.

Gullie's hand shot out to grip the wall. "They need to get inside. Now."

She scowled back at him. "Are you nuts, kid? My soldiers just took a U.S. Air Force jet out of the sky. We can't stop now."

The soldiers in question neared the downed jet, weapons raised as a man crawled out, choking. He looked injured, one leg not moving. One of the soldiers closed in, shouting to him, and the man raised his arms in surrender.

Gullie tugged on Orla's arm to get her attention. "If your men and women don't get inside this village right now, they'll be left behind."

She finally turned to him. "What did you just say?"

"We're taking the village to the fae realm to regroup."

She shook her head. "Leave me alone, boy. We aren't retreating now, not when were so close to finishing this once and for all."

"You're going to finish it in a body sack." He didn't know if that was the right word, and Tia would have most likely corrected him, but right now he didn't care. He wouldn't leave them behind. "Get inside this village. Now." It was an order, one he was sure to catch hell for. "I promise you'll regret it if you don't."

She studied him for a moment before another bomb went off behind them, throwing them onto their hands and knees. Pain seared up Gulliver's arms, and blood seeped through cuts in his palms.

Orla lifted her head and pushed to her feet. "Retreat!" she screamed. "Everyone back inside these walls. Now!"

Soldiers ran toward them, and once Gullie was satisfied they'd make it, he took off for the town square. The shield was still intact over this part of the village, making it quieter than the rest.

Brandon, Griffin, Toby, and Xavier stood ready to make a move.

"It's going to transport us ... with it?" Xavier sounded like he didn't know if that would be better than facing the bombs falling from the sky.

Griff ignored him. "Where are we going?"

"Not Iskalt," Toby and Gullie said at the same time.

"We're coming back," Toby said. "That will be infinitely harder if my sister locks me in the safety of the palace."

Gullie didn't disagree with that. There was no way Tia would send them back into a war. Not like she'd sent Sophie. He'd done his best not to think of her, to wonder where she was, if she watched her father and those like him try to wipe a race of people from their world and turned away.

"Fargelsi means explaining to Neeve why the village is half destroyed." Brandon shook his head. "Eldur it is."

Queen Alona and Finn would provide them with the aid they needed and the repairs to the village without the doubt and chastisement. Without trying to prevent them from returning to protect the rest of the half-fae living in this world.

Brandon started the spell, drawing on his Fargelsian magic that didn't need the sun or the moon as he pushed stones into place. Gullie didn't know how it worked exactly, only that the stones controlled the path of the village and where it would end up.

Fire lit up the dark sky as a building nearby went up in flames. It was the home he'd once stayed in with Tia and Toby as children when they'd hidden from their parents so they wouldn't be sent away from a fight they belonged in. Now, it too was gone.

Just like so many other things.

Brandon's unintelligible words filled the air with a thickness as they simmered like a pot ready to boil over. His muscles shook as he pushed the last stone into place.

Xavier's hand slid into Toby's, and Gullie stepped closer to his father. Something wasn't right. They could all feel it.

"It's so much power," Brandon grit out, his knees collapsing. He fell to the stones. "The village, it's trying."

When he opened his eyes, they were bloodshot and hazy.

"Dad, help him." Gullie shoved Griff toward Brandon.

Griff bent down to help him up. "Take a break and try again."

Brandon shook his head. "I started the spell. I can't stop it now." He whispered a string of words in Fargelsian. "I can only give it more strength from my own magic." He struggled to get the words of magic out through gritted teeth.

Cracks formed in the stone beneath their feet. The damage wasn't from a bomb or any sort of human explosion. No, this was magic.

"Aghadoon is destroying itself." Toby yanked Xavier away from a fissure opening under them.

"Brandon." Griffin shook him. "Come on, old man. Fix this. There has to be a spell in the library to stop it. Tell me which one."

Brandon's breath came in short gasps. "I can't ... hold it."

"What can we do to help?" Toby asked. "Grandfather, tell us what to do."

"Holding the shield ... trying to transport this many people ... Aghadoon is injured. It doesn't have enough magic. The village is dying. I can feel it."

"No." Griff kneeled next to him. "Tell me the spell. I don't have Fargelsian magic, but I know the language. Maybe I can help."

Griff hadn't spoken of his knowledge of Fargelsian in years. He didn't like to think about his years as the mad queen's surrogate son. At least, that was what Gullie's mother told him.

"Me too." Toby moved to their side. "I don't have magic, but I do have Fargelsian blood."

Brandon nodded and started a strengthening spell. "*Lopeta tuho ja ota minulta voima.*"

The other's joined in, repeating the same lines over and over until a crowd formed up and everyone was chanting the Fargelsian words.

"*Lopeta tuho ja ota minulta voima.*"

The ground trembled and an earsplitting crack shrieked through the village as a line ran down the cobblestone street to the nearest building, splitting it in two.

Orla ran toward them. "Everyone is inside," she told Gullie. "You promise me, kid. We're coming back."

He nodded, hardly hearing her words as he watched his father sink lower to the ground, the weight of the village's magic around his neck. Those without magic didn't appear affected, standing straighter, their voices grew louder as they spoke the spell that seemed to give strength to the ancient words.

It was no use.

Brandon fell over and Gullie scrambled to him. "Don't stop. You can't." He wrapped his arms around the older man, willing his defensive magic to give him what he needed.

The shield above them let out a thunderous boom as another rupture ripped through it. Soon, it would be completely down, and they'd be at the mercy of the humans.

Brandon grappled to hold on to Gulliver's arm. "The

village can't hold the shield and transport this many people." His gaze shot past Gullie to his grandson. "But there's another way."

Gullie looked over his shoulder to find that Toby had heard him and was in a battle of wills, his eyes not leaving Brandon's. The old man was right, of course.

It had been over ten years since Toby took an entire army through one of his portals, but he was the only fae to have ever been able to do such a thing. Most O'Sheas could only transport a handful of fae with them.

Even Griff couldn't accomplish such a feat.

But the last time Toby did, it was by force when King Egan held him prisoner.

Griffin lifted his head. "Gullie, you and Toby have to get them out. They're our people. No matter where they choose to live."

"What are they talking about?" Xavier looked from Griff and Brandon to Toby. "If the village can't move, then how ..."

"Toby's magic," Griffin gasped. "It's the only way."

Xavier backed away. "You told me you had no magic."

Toby sighed, a dejected set to his shoulders.

"He doesn't," Gullie blurted. "Well, it's not normal kind of fae magic." Yet, it was the only kind of magic that could save them now.

Chapter Two
SOPHIE

"I'd like to see my father." Sophie crossed her arms over her chest, trying not to let her fear show through the brave facade she had in place. "You know he's a leader of HAFS. He wouldn't want me here." Her words were brave, but she battled to keep her wits about her.

"You know very well your father is the one who brought you here, Sophie-Ann. You will answer my questions first before I allow you to speak with him." Doctor Clarkson pushed back from his dark ebony desk, his arms resting on the soft gray leather of his chair. He'd arrived soon after her, leaving the rest of the HAFS operations in her father's hands, along with a few other chapter leaders like him. But for what? To learn the secrets of the fae? Too bad she wouldn't tell him a thing.

Sophie didn't need a reminder that her father had betrayed her, but there was still a small part of her that couldn't believe he understood what he'd subjected his own daughter to. He was confused.

Despite everything they'd been through, despite all their disagreements and frustrations, Sophie knew her father loved her. It was the fae he hated.

But the fae had saved her life.

Gulliver O'Shea had saved her life. The boy with the kind eyes and the strange tail that she now couldn't imagine him without.

"I don't know what you're talking about." Sophie gave a weary sigh. The drugs they'd pumped into her system since her arrival at the Clarkson Institute left her mind foggy and her body weak. It took everything she had to keep her mind focused, but it was a battle she was losing.

"What magic have you been exposed to, Sophie-Ann?" His penetrating eyes seemed to stare right through her.

"Don't call me that."

"Why not? It's your name, isn't it?" His long, white fingers fluttered like butterflies around his face, but she knew that wasn't right.

Squinting again, she realized his hands were steepled under his chin as he peered at her expectantly.

"My dad calls me Sophie-Ann. Everyone else calls me Sophie."

"Fine, Sophie." He sighed. "Tell me what magic you've been exposed to? What have those fae creatures done to you?"

"Nothing," she muttered, a heavy blanket of confusion settled over her. She couldn't remember why she wanted so desperately not to tell him anything. She had a reason. A good one. It just escaped her at the moment.

"The last time your father saw you in the hospital, you were at death's door. You were missing for weeks. There was no sign of you anywhere until several high-profile fae criminals returned to the human world and brought you with them, fully restored to the picture of health. Can you explain that?"

Sophie shrugged. "They healed me in one of their kingdoms. They were kind and didn't—"

"They took you to their realm?" Doctor Clarkson interrupted her.

Crap. She hadn't meant to give that bit away.

Sophie shrugged again. "They don't want a war with humans."

"They have a funny way of showing it." He scowled. "They have nearly destroyed Los Angeles in their attempt to claim it for themselves."

Sophie ran a hand through her tangled hair. "How long have I been here?"

"Tell me what I need to know, Sophie-Ann." The doctor's voice rose in agitation. "What magic have you been exposed to?"

"I don't know." Her voice grated in equal irritation. "The healing kind." She threw her hands up in defeat.

"You're lying. We've never known them to have healing magic. Try again, Sophie. This time with the truth."

"I told you the truth already, but you don't want to hear it." Her voice came out like a whine. His questions were exhausting and all she wanted was to curl up somewhere—anywhere—and go back to sleep.

"You look like Sophie-Ann Devereaux. You sound like her." Doctor Clarkson's fist slammed down on his elegantly polished desk, making her jump to attention, all thoughts of sleep vanished with her racing heart. "But they've done something to you, haven't they? They've changed you."

"Are you trying to say I'm a changeling?" She scowled. "That's not how that works. Queen Brea was a changeling. They swapped her with Queen Alona when they were babies. To protect them."

"Queen Brea?" His jaw dropped. "You don't mean Brea Robinson?"

"No. I don't know. You're confusing me." She was too tired to answer more questions. Sophie just wanted to return to her room and escape into the arms of a blissful, dreamless sleep. That was all she seemed to want to do since she'd arrived at the institute.

"Focus, Sophie. What did they do to you?"

"They saved my life." Her hands clenched into fists as she fought to keep her wits about her. She didn't want to give anything away that might hurt Gullie or his family. The fae were kind to her. They'd kept every promise they made, and she didn't want to betray them.

"How?"

"You know very well they have magic, Doctor."

"What kind of magic?" he pressed. "We know some have magic fueled by the sun, and others with moonlight. We know those with day magic are powerless at night. We know some have magic all the time, but it is a weaker magic fueled by the earth and some ancient powerful language. And the cursed darkness we experienced comes from the evil beast-like creatures who have no magic of their own."

Sophie blinked. "You know a lot more than I do, then."

"None of them have the power to heal leukemia in its final stages!" Spittle flew from the doctor's mouth, and his eye grew wild with fury.

Sophie shrank back in her chair, desperate to escape this

nightmare she'd found herself in. "It's new magic," she blurted. "New to some of them, I guess, but it's ancient magic they don't seem to know what to do with."

"But they went to the trouble of kidnapping you from your deathbed to take you to their world? Were they experimenting on you?"

"No, of course not."

"Where did this magic come from? Where did they find it?"

"It's not that simple." She rubbed her eyes and fidgeted in her seat.

"Tell me what I want to know and you can go back to your rooms. I'll even have the nurses bring you a special meal. Something you'll enjoy."

The food at the Clarkson Institute bordered on abuse. Most days, she got bland, pasty oatmeal for breakfast, cheap bologna sandwiches for lunch, and most often, an indecipherable stew for dinner with hard rolls.

The mention of decent food had her stomach growling in anticipation.

"You like Thai food?"

Her mouth watered at the thought of her favorite curry chicken and basil fried rice with cashews and pineapple.

"Where does this healing magic come from?" Clarkson demanded.

"Lenya," Sophie whispered, hating herself for the betrayal. But it wasn't like the humans could travel there anyway.

"And where is that?"

"In their world. They've only recently discovered the people of Lenya, who lived on the other side of a place they called the fire plains. There were two small kingdoms separated from the others for thousands of years. Their magic is different from the others."

"And your fae friends took you there?"

Sophie nodded. A splash of something wet landed on her hand. It took her a moment to realize she was crying.

"How did they heal you?"

"A pool. I was moments from death, and the waters of the healing pools of Lenya saved me."

"Why you?" he demanded. "From what we know of the fae, they don't take too kindly to humans. So, why would one of them bother to help a human?"

"I don't know."

Clarkson didn't need to know how many rules Gulliver probably broke to save her the way he had.

"All I know is that they were kind to me."

"You are a naïve girl if you believe them capable of anything resembling kindness." He shook his head. "When you let them touch you with their magic, you become their creature. No longer human, but not quite fae."

"That's ludicrous. I'm still me. And for the record, they treated me far better than you have, Doctor Clarkson."

"Tell me, if you're still human, still you, then why have you turned your back on your own kind in favor of your new masters?" He leaned across the desk, his eyes boring into hers.

"They aren't my masters. And I haven't turned my back on humans. I just ... I believe there is a way we can coexist if we learn to understand each other. They have a strange perception of humans. Almost childlike."

The doctor stood from his seat, a sad look on his face. "You might be a lost cause, Sophie-Ann Devereaux, but I promised your father I would try to bring you back. And I will."

"What does that mean?" She watched him move to the door to call one of the orderlies she despised. They were the worst sort of caregivers one could imagine.

"We are done for the day." He waved two men into the

office. "Take her back to her room and see that she gets a treat for dinner. Unlike the fae, I keep my promises."

Sophie didn't try to argue with him as the two men dressed in white scrubs led her from the room. In her experience, the fae kept their promises far better than most humans.

Sophie shuffled down the hall between the orderlies. The short walk from her therapy session to her room left her exhausted. She hadn't felt this weak since before she entered the hospital for the last time, when she thought she'd never leave it.

As she sank down onto her bed, she wondered if death might find her here in this awful place. Like it was circling back around for her again after narrowly missing her the first time.

"Cooperate, Miss Devereaux," the big orderly snapped at her, yanking her hand forward and dumping several pills into it.

"I am." She pulled her hand back, giving him her best glare. She wasn't sure how scary it could be considering her eyes crossed and he went all fuzzy around the edges. "I just didn't hear you." She popped the pills in her mouth, having learned it was futile to resist the drugs they shoved down her throat—literally, when she didn't cooperate.

Somewhere in the back of her mind, she knew she was never going to get out of this mess if she didn't have her wits about her, but her head was so full of fog that she couldn't find the desire to care.

"Swallow." The orderly shoved a paper cup of water into her hand, and she gulped the pills down. At least they would send her into a dreamless sleep soon.

"Leave the poor girl alone." The nurse with the pretty lavender eyes chased the orderlies out of the tiny room that wasn't much better than a prison cell. "Idiots," she muttered under her breath as she rolled a cart into the room.

Sophie sat on the edge of her bed waiting for the nurse to take her vitals.

"I'm sorry they've been so hard on you since you got here." She took Sophie's blood pressure, temperature, and pulse. "You'd think they'd have learned by now that you get a lot further with a little kindness and a patient hand." She smoothed the dirty hair back from Sophie's face. "I bet a shower would make you feel better."

Sophie shrugged. The thought of putting forth the effort to take a shower left her even more exhausted. "Maybe tomorrow. I'm too tired tonight."

"That's what you said last night, hon." She buzzed around the room, refilling Sophie's water and fluffing her pillows. "At least tonight you get the good food." She beamed a stunning smile at Sophie, and something about her seemed familiar. But the thought was fleeting.

"Let's get you comfortable and in bed." She helped Sophie ease back onto the lumpy mattress and raised the head so she could sit up to eat dinner.

Sophie's stomach grumbled at the thought of Thai food from some local hot spot, but when the nurse pulled her tray from the cart and set it in front of her, she wanted to cry. It was Thai food, of a sort.

"It's actually not that bad," the woman said, responding to the look on Sophie's face.

It was some sort of frozen dinner of chicken curry and rice with vegetables. They even put a fortune cookie on her plate next to one of those tiny cans of Coke that contained two or three sips.

"Trust me, it's better than the beef stroganoff surprise." The nurse laughed. "The surprise is that it's not beef."

Sophie cracked a smile for the chatty lady. "What's

happening out there?" She blurted the question before she thought better of it.

"In the common room? The same as always. A repeat of one familiar movie or another. You won't miss anything important if you stay in your room tonight."

"No. Out there." She pointed toward the barred clerestory windows high above her bed.

"Nothing to worry about right now. You should eat your dinner and turn in early. You'll feel better tomorrow."

"You said that last night." Sophie sighed. She was so out of touch with what was happening between the fae and the humans. If it weren't for Clarkson's constant questions about the fae, she would probably think it was all just a figment of her imagination.

Maybe it was. Maybe she didn't travel from her home in New Orleans through a portal to a far-off fantasy land. Maybe Sophie Devereaux really was crazy.

That would make more sense than a magical race of fairies who healed her leukemia moments before her death.

"And don't forget your fortune cookie," the nurse reminded her. "That's the best part." She gave Sophie a final grin and left her to her fake Thai meal.

She ate as much of the bland food as she could stomach before she pushed her tray away. As her eyes drooped, she remembered the fortune cookie.

Sophie and her dad used to love sharing their fortunes after a meal of Thai takeout. Tears blurred her vision as she cracked open the cookie and pulled out the slip of paper to see what words of wisdom were there to cheer her up.

Don't lose hope, Sophie-Ann.

Chapter Three
GULLIVER

"Everyone, move!" Griff yelled, ushering half-fae toward the portal Toby held open.

Rock sprayed from above as another missile sailed through the night sky to find its target. Yet, those surrounding them, the ones who'd been fighting the humans and running from explosions only moments ago, now looked scared.

Toby sighed, looking at Xavier with urgency. There was a new distrust in Xavier's eyes, yet he still turned to the others. "Trust them. We have no choice."

It was then Gulliver realized the truth. The half-fae were at odds with the humans, but the fae were completely foreign to them.

At Xavier's insistence, their warriors ran toward the portal, disappearing into it. Toby's magic would guide them to the right destination. No one had more control over the O'Shea power than he did.

But Gulliver didn't want to go with them. Not when Griff was staying behind. He looked to his father, saw the blood streaking down his face, the soot dulling his auburn hair.

Griff met his gaze. "I'll meet you there."

There was no guarantee of that. The village was damaged from the constant barrage of attacks. Even now, thunderous booms shook the ground. Unlike the fae who were running out of strength, the humans and their machines could go all night. Gulliver stumbled, and a hand gripped his arm. It was Brandon, the strangest and most mysterious fae he'd ever met. Tia's and Toby's grandfather also had the answers to every question they'd ever asked.

"The humans won't have this village, Gulliver." His intense gaze was enough to burn a hole right through any magic. "Your father will be safe."

"Gullie," Toby yelled. "I can't hold it open much longer."

Gulliver glanced around, realizing he was one of the last remaining in the square. Without looking back, he stepped into the portal. The magic drew him in, a familiar feeling. Unlike the portal that dropped him in Lenya, this one didn't have any chaos about it.

Toby was not his sister. He lacked every ounce of her unpredictability, and his magic reflected that. It was a clear and peaceful route to Eldur. The ground rushed up at him and he braced for the impact—stone instead of the soft grass of the farmhouse in the human realm.

Daylight filled the portal seconds before Gulliver crashed

onto the cobblestones, his knees buckling with the impact and he staggered forward to regain his balance.

The others groaned from where they'd landed flat on their backs.

"Everyone okay?" He shielded his eyes from the overbearing sun of an Eldurian afternoon as he searched for anyone who needed help.

Xavier got up on his hands and knees, the full contents of his stomach spewing out of his mouth.

Where was Toby?

Turning, Gulliver couldn't find him, but he froze when he noticed where they were. Radur City. Toby had landed them right on the doorstep of the palace, and they weren't alone.

A crowd of Eldurians stared at them, the crescendo of their alarm ringing on the wind.

One voice rose above the rest, amplified by magic. "I seem to have lost your attention." Alona, the Queen of Eldur was giving a speech, probably from the gardens above the canyon city. She couldn't have seen their arrival from up there. "It happens. I can be very boring." When no one laughed, she went on. "Come on, that was a good joke."

Gulliver heard the influence of Brea in her voice. The two semi-sisters were close, and just hearing her sent relief flooding him. They were safe. He was home. It might not have been Iskalt or Myrkur, but Alona and Finn were family too.

"Hello?" Irritation entered her voice now. "What has trapped your attention more than my boring matters of state?"

The back of the crowd seemed to gather their wits about them and realized there were fae who needed help. The Eldurians had always been known as a welcoming people. They converged on them, and Gulliver caught the frantic looks of the half-fae.

"Xavier, where's Toby?"

Xavier heaved in a breath. "I don't know." He blinked rapidly in the sunlight. "How is it day? Have we been unconscious?" His voice cracked like he was close to panic. "What have you done to us?"

"Relax." Gulliver laid a hand on his shoulder. "There is a difference in time between our worlds. Whenever it is night in the human realm, it is day here."

"Oh." He nodded, still looking a bit stunned.

"Orla," Gulliver called on their leader. "Calm everyone down. No one here will hurt you. You're safe now." He explained the shock of daylight to her and others nearby began spreading the word.

"Forgive me, Gulliver," she said, arms crossed over her chest. "But we aren't safe anywhere. You remember the bombs back there, right? We can't go from dodging bombs at night to staring down a mob in broad daylight and feel any kind of safety." She backed away from the crowd, putting herself between the Eldurians and her fae.

New tactic. Gulliver stepped toward the crowd. "We're friends. Please stay back. They're frightened."

The crowd parted with hushed whispers as a figure rushed through the gathering, stopping when he saw Gulliver.

"Finn." Gulliver's heart hitched at the sight of someone familiar. Family. And more importantly, an adulty-adult who could handle this situation far better than he could.

"Gulliver?" He shook his head. "What have you done?" He looked past Gulliver to the half-fae, most of whom still appeared human even in the fae realm. "Humans, really?" He rubbed his eyes. "As if the girl wasn't bad enough." His voice lifted on his magic. "It's okay, Lona. Gulliver is here."

"Gulliver?" Princess Darra's magic or one of the queen's guards must have amplified her voice since she had none of her own. "What's he doing here?"

"Well, I'm not really sure, but I was just about to ask him."

"Stop talking to me then and just do it."

They seemed oblivious to the fact that the entire crowd who'd come to hear the queen now listened to their conversation.

Finn lifted an eyebrow, placing one hand on the hilt of his sword as Xavier and Orla walked up behind Gulliver. "You heard her. Care to tell me why you've brought humans to Eldur? Am I to assume Tia is behind this? It smells like her."

Worry gnawed at Gulliver. Toby still hadn't appeared. Had something happened in the village? He needed to get back to the human realm to find him, but his cousin wasn't the only one he'd left behind.

Sophie was somewhere among her father's men, the ones attacking his fae.

He shook his head. "It was Toby."

"Then, where is he?" Finn's eyes widened. "Gulliver, if you lost Brea's child..." He swallowed heavily. Toby was more than Brea's kid to Finn. He was the last part of Logan in this world. The two of them hadn't existed separately since they were fourteen years old.

"We have to go back." Xavier looked over his shoulder. "We can't abandon him."

Tears gathered in Gulliver's eyes, but he blinked them away. "The only fae who could take us back is Toby."

"What do you mean?"

"Finn." Alona spoke again. "What's happening? Give me the blow by blow."

That was a Brea phrase, and Gulliver wiped his eyes at the sound of it. "Don't tell her. Please. Not yet."

Finn lifted his voice. "Just having a nice Sunday morning chat with a friend, love."

Gulliver laughed, despite the panic building in his chest.

Xavier and Orla were arguing about something, but he paid them no attention. It didn't matter what they thought or if they felt safe. No one here would hurt them, and Gullie had never been happier to be in the fae realm.

It hit him all at once. The battle. The race to save the half-fae from a fight they couldn't win. The near destruction of Aghadoon. Leaving his father and Brandon behind. Sophie. It was too much. Gulliver lunged forward, wrapping a surprised Finn in a hug, his hands shaking.

Finn pressed Gulliver's head into his chest. "It's okay, kid." Gulliver might have been in his twenties, but he'd never minded anyone treating him younger because it was out of affection. "Whatever happened is over now. You're here."

Gulliver could still see them. The bombs, the fire raging through the sacred village. Would Aghadoon ever be the same? He couldn't seem to stop shaking.

"Take a deep breath, Gullie. You're safe now." His voice lifted magically as he turned to the crowd of stunned half-fae. "You're all safe now." To Gulliver, he asked. "What in the five kingdoms has happened?"

"My father," he said into Finn's shirt, "he's still back there with Brandon and Toby. There was a war." He pulled away. "These aren't humans, Finn. Well, not entirely. They're half-fae."

"Finn, bring Gullie to me right this minute." Alona was starting to sound irritated, but her husband stood frozen, staring at the dozens of half-fae who'd backed as far away from the crowd as they could. They had gathered in a far corner of the road running along the edge of the river canyon. Some peered down over the railing to the lower regions of the city.

A scream echoed off the nearby shops, the very cobblestones themselves, as Darra came running through the crowd. The Eldurian heir was a beautiful young woman, only seventeen, who was also a little wild. Instead of the corseted dress that fit her position, she wore a long flowing blue skirt and tunic shirt. Her hair was down and threaded with white flowers.

She collided with Gulliver before he could even register her presence. "Tia wrote to me that you'd gone to the human realm." She leaned back, studying him. "You're too good for the likes of them, Gul. Too kind." All she knew of humans were the stories from Brea of the treatment she'd received.

"I'm okay." He attempted a smile, but the anxiety churning within him pulled it taught. "I..."

"Who opened the portal? Is Toby or Griff here?"

Tears finally escaped his eyes, and he collapsed against her, his body shaking. "I failed everyone." His father. Toby. Sophie. He was here in safety with a bunch of half-fae, who looked like they'd rather be anywhere else, while the ones he cared about fought the humans.

The blazing desert sun beat down on them, not so different from the heat they'd experienced in L.A.

"Someone tell me what's going on!" Alona was yelling now. They could tell even with magic amplifying her voice.

Darra's lips twitched. "Mom had to wear her most constricting dress today."

"Had to?" Finn asked.

"Okay, she chose it. You know how she is. Well, to get down here without a trail of guards, I had to climb, and she's just salty she couldn't do the same."

"Say it again." Gulliver sighed. "Say *salty*." It was one of Tia's favorite humanisms.

Darra's smile faded. "You'll see her soon enough now that you're back." She looped her arm through his. "We'll find Toby. I promise. And Griff. We can get word to Uncle Lochlan. I think he's in Iskalt at the moment. Probably at his hunting lodge"

It would be too late, but he didn't say that. Instead, he nodded, wishing it could be true.

The crowd started running, and Gulliver turned to see what had them sprinting back toward the palace. A bright light rent the air, almost like an explosion, the kind he'd become all too familiar with. For a moment, the air shimmered and they could see through to the human realm, to the battle of Aghadoon. Artillery fire blasted through the village, exploding through the portal and into Eldur, bullets licking up the stone face of a nearby tavern.

Screams rang out in the street, and the half-fae readied themselves to fight, even in their confusion and exhaustion.

A plane soared above Aghadoon, the likes of which the fae of Eldur had never seen. And then, it was gone, as if the opening had never been there to begin with. It left a trail of fire across the sky, and one lone figure.

Toby wobbled on his feet at the center of Radur city. The hem of his shirt was singed, but he looked unharmed. That was, until Gullie noticed the blood trickling from his ear.

Gullie ran toward him, but he wasn't fast enough. Before anyone could help him, Toby's legs crumpled beneath him and his body crashed into the street.

Chapter Four
TOBY

Ringing filled his ears where a moment ago there had been nothing but blissful silence and darkness. Fire, he remembered the fire and his grandfather being trapped by it, forcing him to close his portal to help. Then came the explosions. One after another in a symphony lighting up the night.

Griffin had made him leave. Toby tried to refuse, but Aghadoon was as good as gone. In those last moments, Griffin had forced him to leave them behind.

He almost hadn't been able to get another portal open, and the moment Toby stepped into it, an explosion tore it wide open. It took everything he had to hold it together, to prevent it from creating another rift between the worlds. By the time his feet touched down in Eldur, he'd had nothing left.

Rough cobblestone scratched at his back, and his eyes were crusted shut, but he forced them open, one then the other. Many faces hovered over him in the hot Eldur afternoon, but there was only one he wanted to see. Darra. She was here, looking so much like her brother it both broke and healed something inside him.

She smiled down at him, that front tooth slightly crooked like Logan's had been. "Hi, stranger."

He hadn't been able to set foot in Eldur since Logan died. It was too hard, but he was ready now. Ready to do whatever he needed to for the fae living in the human realm.

"I brought some friends!" he shouted over the ringing in his ears.

She laughed, tears shining in her eyes. "I can see that. You always were one for trouble."

"I think you're confusing me with my sister." It was then he noticed the other faces. Finn wore a sad smile. Gulliver looked like he was going to throw up. And Xavier ... Toby couldn't decipher the way he looked at him now.

"You don't need to shout, Tobes, we can hear you," Darra said.

"Someone want to help me up?" He lifted a brow. "Or I can just lay here in the street and go back to sleep."

"Everyone back up," Alona yelled over Toby, walking toward them through the crowd. "Give the Iskaltian prince some space."

"Look who finally decided to make her way down." Darra rolled her eyes.

There was a rough slit cut up Alona's dress, almost like she'd ripped it herself to loosen it.

"Your Majesty!" A guard ran toward her in the traditional Eldur livery.

"What is it?" Alona stepped toward him as he stopped to catch his breath.

"Aghadoon has been set down just outside the city near the orchards."

"What'd he say about Aghadoon?" Toby shared a look with Gulliver, who was blinking away tears. "They made it?" The ringing in his ears seemed to get louder and louder. "Well, what are we waiting for?"

Gulliver reached down to help him up, and Darra grabbed him under his other arm.

"Absolutely not." Alona crossed her arms. "Toby needs to get to the healer. Gulliver, you and Finn will go to Aghadoon."

"I'm not going to the palace when my grandfather and uncle might be hurt!" Toby tried to hide his limp, but he knew he wasn't fooling anyone.

Darra looked back at her mother. "It's his choice, Mom."

"This next generation of fae royals is going to drive us all into early graves." But she didn't try to stop them again. Instead, she commandeered three horses from her guards. Toby rode with Finn, who helped keep him upright. Darra and Gulliver each got their own.

Traveling on horseback through a city with no odd magic-like electricity or giant cars felt right, and yet, Toby missed the constant energy of the human realm, the way they never seemed to stop moving. There, they didn't need fae magic to have value.

He'd left Xavier behind with Alona, who he knew would make sure everyone got the help they needed.

By the time they reached the outer city limits, they saw it. The pillars of Aghadoon were half crumbled into dust, the remaining stones sticking up like reminders of the beauty they'd once held.

The high walls bore the marks of battle. Holes in the stone that would need repairs. Black burns stretched across the surface. But it was the village within that suffered the most damage.

Two figures emerged from the dust, walking toward Radur City.

Gulliver slid from his mount, ran toward his father, and wrapped him in a long hug.

Finn helped Toby down, and he refused assistance walking toward his grandfather.

"I shouldn't have asked you to come." It was what hurt the most. As much as he wanted to help their half-fae brethren, it put the fae's most sacred place at risk.

His grandfather put a hand under his chin and tilted it up. "I knew the risk, Toby. It is my guilt to bear, not yours. I did not imagine what it would come to, but when my grandson has need of me, I will come. Always." His smile reached all the way to his tired eyes. "We were worried when that explosion hit just as your portal closed."

"I can only somewhat hear you, but I'm okay." He knew there was probably still blood on his face, he could feel it trickling from his ear, but he didn't want to worry anyone. "I promise. I'm just so relieved you both made it back in one piece."

Finn cleared his throat. "I think it's about time we learned what's going on. I'm not surprised you two are involved in this." He looked from the half-destroyed Aghadoon to Brandon and Griff.

"Yes." Darra nodded eagerly. "Why were there humans sprawled all over our street during Mom's speech?"

A group of horses galloped toward them from the city, stopping when they came close. Four guards who had most likely been sent by Alona.

The first one nudged his horse forward. "We are to escort you to the palace."

Toby rolled his eyes. He was well versed in queen behavior from his mom and sister. They were impatient and thought they deserved all information before others.

"May as well go." Darra slipped his arm over her shoulder to help him. "You won't get out of it."

All Toby wanted was to have a bath, a hot meal, get his ears to stop ringing, and then plan how they were going to defeat the humans and help the rest of the fae and half-fae in the human realm.

Yet, he knew the routine. First, he had a queen to talk to.

The guards led them through the streets that were teeming with curious Eldurians. The half-fae were nowhere to be seen, but that didn't worry Toby. They'd be cared for here.

The Eldurian palace was a maze of halls, interspersed with courtyards that featured grand fountains and beautiful gardens. They favored anything that let them sit outside among shade trees and cool water.

Toby couldn't help thinking of the last time he'd been here. It was a visit for Logan's nineteenth name day. Tia was missing, so neither of them felt much like celebrating. Instead, they sat together under the stars, wondering if his sister looked up at the same sky.

He'd never imagined he would get his sister back but lose Logan.

They passed the entrance to the residence wing on their way to the throne room, and Toby looked away. For the past couple of months, he'd managed to push Logan's memories from tragic loss into fond remembrance. Xavier's friendship helped him want to live again. He stopped wishing he'd been taken with the man he loved.

Yet, now, he was back right where he'd started.

Almost as if he could read his mind, Brandon set a hand on Toby's back. His grandfather's presence had always been comforting, a symbol of safety. The man had been through too much for anything to scare him, and his steadiness made those around him swell with courage.

The ornate mahogany doors to the throne room stood open, and Alona sat on her wooden throne, her foot tapping anxiously. Before her, Xavier and Orla shifted uncomfortably.

Darra stopped next to Xavier, still holding Toby up.

"What are you doing here?" Toby hissed. He couldn't look at Xavier in this palace, in front of these people. Shame flooded him at the way he'd let Xavier push Alona's son further into the back of his mind.

Xavier shifted away from him, almost as if Toby frightened him now. "Orla and I are representing the half-fae."

"So, it's true?" Darra asked. "Those people out there are half-fae? They look so human."

Xavier nodded. "Some of them are fae entirely, but that is rare for those living in the human realm. Our ancestors have intermarried with humans for generations."

Alona slapped a hand on the arm of her throne. "Will someone tell me what is going on?"

Everyone was looking at Toby, even Gulliver and Griff, to explain. None of them wanted to tell Alona of Tia's plan.

He let go of Darra. "I need to sit down." A page boy quickly brought over a velvet chair, and Toby sat. "Tia started hearing rumblings of a group in the human realm targeting fae."

"Why is he shouting?" Alona darted a worried look around the room. "What's wrong with him?"

"One of the human bombs exploded in his ear. He'll be

okay soon. The ringing wears off after a while." Griffin clapped him on the back.

Alona nodded. "We were aware of Tia's suspicions. Our agreement was to wait and watch."

"But it's Tia."

She sighed. "Brea's daughter through and through. What did she do?"

Gulliver's tail wrapped around his middle almost like a protective shield. "She sent me to the human realm to investigate."

"I was sent with him because she wanted me out of the palace." Toby shrugged. It was the truth. "But what we learned was worse than expected. Fae and half-fae were not only being targeted by bombings ... err ... explosions in New Orleans, but in other cities as well."

"The group is called the Human Alliance for Survival." Gulliver lifted his gaze to the queen. "They think our very existence in their world threatens theirs."

"But we do not want to harm them." Alona looked as confused as Toby had been at first.

"No, but our magic is a threat to them," Toby explained. "At least, they think it is. Most half-fae have little power to speak of. Yet, the humans would still eradicate them."

"It got worse when I sort of abducted a HAFS leader's daughter." Gulliver's voice was low, almost inaudible.

But Alona heard it because she lurched forward out of her throne. "Excuse me?"

They explained the rest to her about the healing pools, bringing Aghadoon to the human realm as a haven, the attack. And then, the portal bringing them to Eldur.

Alona, Darra, and Finn were entranced by the story and also seemingly horrified. They ended on the fact that the human realm was now at war with the fae, and it wouldn't end. At least, not right away.

The fae could no longer stay out of this fight.

When they were finished, Alona went to speak with a maid about making up rooms for their guests. Xavier approached Toby. "Camp has been set up for our people outside the city. I'm going to stay there." His eyes traveled around their opulent settings like he didn't trust any of it.

"What?" He leaned closer to Xavier. "Oh, camp? Yes! That's a good idea." Despite his raised voice, Toby kept all emotion out of his tone. Once the half-fae were gone, his shoulders drooped.

Gulliver's tail tapped his back in reassurance. "This must be hard for him. Going from the human realm to one of their fairy tales."

Toby shrugged. "Sure." He had no more energy for all things Xavier, not while he sat in Logan's home.

The palace healer insisted Toby needed rest, but he didn't want to stay in the infirmary. Gulliver and Darra promised to watch over him and they were allowed to take him to Darra's chambers as long as Griffin accompanied them.

It was like old times. They sat enjoying freshly baked bread, deep red Eldurian wine, and the sharpest Fargelsian cheese, with ripe shadow berries from Myrkur, along with smoked fish from Iskalt, and sweet iced chocoah from Lenya for dessert. A feast of the five kingdoms, Darra called it.

As hungry as Toby was, he only picked at his food. He could feel Darra, Gulliver, and Griff watching him, waiting for him to break. But he wasn't his sister. He wouldn't let the entire world into his heart to learn what contents it held. His grief was his own.

After they'd eaten in silence for a while, Griff spoke up. "I'm leaving tonight."

Toby saw Gulliver snap his eyes to his father. "You can't. I ... Dad ..."

Griff reached for his hand. "It's okay, Gul. I'm here. We all made it out of there. I'm just going to Iskalt to fetch Tia. She should be here. I'll travel to the farmhouse and then on to Iskalt. The humans won't even know I'm there."

Toby let them have their moment and focused on Griff's words. He would bring Tia here, and there was nothing Toby needed more than his sister. For so long, he'd kept her at arm's length, maybe blaming her on some level for Logan's death. He'd treated her terribly, hadn't helped in the first year of her reign.

Yet, she would still come. Because she was Tia and he was Toby. No matter what, they'd always save each other.

Chapter Five
SOPHIE

Sophie shuffled down the wide hallway, the dingy vinyl floors a stark contrast against her cheap white slippers. Fluorescent lights flickered overhead as she passed door after door, each closed to conceal the inmate ... patient ... behind the small shatterproof windows.

She was finally free. Sort of. She'd earned the privilege to visit the dining hall and common room without escort. And she'd traded in her hospital gown for blue pajama-like scrubs and a threadbare white robe. Today was her first chance to explore, and so far, Sophie didn't like what she saw.

Since her arrival at the Clarkson Institute, she'd been

heavily drugged and too incoherent to take stock of her surroundings. She was still drugged, and her mind was foggy, but she no longer felt like she was underwater.

But she was weak and confused. And she needed answers. How had her own father allowed her to be taken to such a place? Sophie stood in the doorway to the dining hall, appalled to see just how many people were housed within the creepy walls of this place. It looked like a horror show. A relic of a bygone era, where unwanted people disappeared behind the walls of an asylum never to be seen again.

Her father wouldn't do that to her, would he?

She picked up a tray from one of the friendlier orderlies passing out meals to the inmates.

Patients.

Shaking her head to clear the fog, she tried to remember she wasn't in a prison, though it felt like. She moved to sit at a table by herself.

Too many other patients looked utterly defeated as they stared blankly at the walls and ceilings, or laughed softly to themselves.

Glancing down at her breakfast tray, Sophie was pleased to see a single pancake. It was the frozen kind meant for toaster ovens, and it was mostly cold, but there was butter and syrup to go with it and what looked like a scoop of powdered eggs and a carton of apple juice. A hunk of some meat-like substance occupied one corner of the tray. It was cut to make it look like ham, but she suspected it was something else.

Her stomach rumbled angrily as she poured syrup over her pancake. It wasn't much, but it was better than the pasty plain oatmeal she'd grown accustomed to since her arrival. She wasn't even sure when that was. It seemed like just a few days, but time was a confusing thing here.

"It's about time you showed up." A little boy climbed into the chair beside her, a carton of apple juice clutched in his hand. His eyes were hollow and sunken with dark circles and a sallow look about his complexion that said he didn't get much time outside.

"Um. Hi." Sophie glanced over her shoulder to make sure the kid was actually speaking to her. She had a fleeting thought about whether the boy was really there or if her mind was playing tricks on her.

"I thought you might have decided to stay wherever you went when you disappeared, but then I saw you in that place. Nurse said it was called California."

"What?" Sophie blinked rapidly, taking in the boy's appearance. Despite his pale skin and shadows under his eyes, he looked better than most of the other patients. His eyes were clear and bright—a golden amber color she couldn't ever remember seeing before.

"I've never been there, but Nurse says it's a pretty place. Sunny, with beaches. I don't know what a beach is, but I'd love to see one someday."

His voice pulsed in her ears, and Sophie swayed in her chair.

"Who are you?" she managed to whisper.

"Dunno." He sipped from his juice box. "I don't have a name."

She blinked again, forcing her attention on the boy when it seemed to want to focus on anything else. His dark blond hair was cut short without much thought for style. He was small, but she imagined he was probably around ten years old. There was something inherently endearing about him. An innocence Sophie found oddly familiar.

"How do you not have a name?" she finally asked.

"Never got a real one." He shrugged as though it was no big

deal. "Some of the nicer nurses call me August, but that's just the month I came here. Most everyone else calls me Patient Eighty-seven."

"How long have you been here?"

"Always." He leaned toward her plate, eyeing it with interest. "Are you going to eat your ham?"

"That's not ham." Sophie wrinkled her nose, shoving her plate toward him. "Help yourself."

"I like it." He took a big bite. "The orderlies usually sneak me an extra piece when it's available, but they were short today."

This poor kid had grown up in the institute. No one had even bothered to give him a decent name, and he thought a slice of fake canned meat was a treat. Sophie felt an overwhelming impulse to protect this child.

He looked up at her with wide golden eyes that seemed to see everything about her. "Where did you go? I missed you."

Sophie frowned at him, her head tilting to get a better look at him through bleary eyes. "Do you know me?" She couldn't place him, but he seemed to believe they were friends.

"Of course. You're the girl I've been waiting for." He took another bite of the not-ham, smacking his lips. "But you left for a long time. And you were really sick, but when you got home, you were different. Healthy and ... scared, I think." He cocked his head at her. "How are you still alive?"

"Well, that's a long story." She glanced around the dining hall to see if anyone was watching their exchange. "How do you know me?"

She was missing something. Her head throbbed, and it felt ten sizes too big for her shoulders. The drugs kept her docile and confused. Something tugged at her memory. Something about this kid.

"I've always known you." He leaned close, dropping his

voice to a whisper. "I dream about you all the time." He pressed a chubby finger over his lips. "But don't tell the doctor about it. He doesn't like it when I do weird stuff. And you shouldn't tell him when you dream about me."

He thought she dreamed about him? What would make him think that?

"Are you half-fae?" Sophie asked, but the mesmerizing quality of his eyes told her that much was true. But why would a half-fae child in a mental institution dream about her?

"Dunno." He shrugged again. "What's a fae?"

"Never mind." She rubbed her eyes and almost expected him not to be there when she opened them again.

"You have to quit the pills. They mess with your head." The boy gave her an intense look, an expression far beyond his years.

"They make me take them." If she could figure out a way to avoid the medication, she would, but the orderlies were thorough.

"They make you stick out your tongue and open your mouth, but they don't check everywhere. Next time, tuck the pills between your upper gums and your cheeks before you drink anything. Once they leave, stick them under your mattress until you get a chance to flush them."

"That's what you do?" Sophie marveled at the boy's ingenuity.

"You have to pretend you're still taking them." He scooted closer to her. "Just drag your feet and mumble a lot. Act confused and slow to understand things, and they'll never know you're not taking them."

"I'll try it, thanks."

"You can't trust the doctor. He's bad."

"I've figured that much."

"Or the orderlies and most of the nurses. You can only trust me and the nurse with the pretty eyes." He slipped off the edge of the chair. "Remember that, okay? Just me and the nice nurse who changes your bed linens."

"The one with the lavender eyes?" She was the only one Sophie had met that could be considered nice.

"Yes. She's good." He started to leave.

"Wait, I have more questions." Sophie turned toward him, lowering her voice. "Can you help me get out of here?"

The boy shook his head, his eyes darkening with sadness. "There's no way out of here." He laid a hand on her shoulder and frowned. "What's your name?"

"You seem to know me, but you don't know my name?"

"I know your face, and I can tell you're good in here." He tapped a finger over his heart.

"I'm Sophie."

The boy nodded, as if her name somehow made sense to him.

"Patient Eighty-seven, you're late." A familiar voice swept across the dining hall, sending everyone into total silence.

Doctor Clarkson marched across the room and grabbed the boy's arm. "You know the punishment for being late for therapy."

Sophie lunged out of her seat. "It's my fault. I kept him with my questions."

"Go." He pointed to the doorway of the dining hall, and the boy sprinted through the double doors. The doctor turned his hateful glare on Sophie, and she winced as she returned to her seat.

"See that you don't delay my patients in the future. We run a tight schedule around here."

"Yes, sir." Sophie whimpered under his scrutiny. She kept

her eyes on her lap until he left through the doors and the din of conversation returned.

"Don't trust them, Sophie." The boy's voice echoed behind her, and she turned just in time to see his pale face disappear through the doors once again.

Chapter Six
GULLIVER

"I need to get back, Tobes." Gulliver paced across the narrow infirmary room. "I'm worried about Sophie. She's surrounded by the enemy."

"What?" Toby shouted. "Gul. Speak up." He rubbed the side of his face, where the healers had bandaged his ear with a potion that reeked of the volcanic mud from Eldfal. Despite Griffin's assurance that Toby's hearing would come back to him soon, the ringing in his ears still hadn't stopped, and Alona had sent him to the infirmary.

"You're really loud." Gulliver moved closer to the bed. "Did the human magic really break your ears?"

Toby nodded. "I got too close to the Aghadoon shields when one of their bombs hit."

"That's why I need to get back." Gulliver leaned closer as he yelled. "Sophie needs me." He pointed at himself, dragging out each syllable.

"It's too dangerous, Gul. I know she's important to you. If anyone gets that, it's me. But we have to figure out our next moves first."

"She might not have time!" Gulliver dropped down onto the bed beside Toby. "She's so strong, but she can be too kind sometimes. I worry what they might do to her if they find out where she's been."

Toby touched his arm. "She'll be okay."

Gulliver turned to face him, speaking slowly so he wouldn't miss a word. "You don't know that. You, of all people, have to understand. If it was Logan back there all alone, would you let anything stop you from getting to him as fast as one of your portals could take you?"

Toby's eyes dropped to his lap. "You're right. But Logan wasn't human. Sophie is, and she's in her own world now, and her father is right there with her. You have to trust that she can take care of herself."

"I know she can." Gulliver dropped his head into his hands. "It's me that can't stand the thought of what she might be going through because of her association with me. I never should have gone looking for food at her cafe."

"You and I both know that's not how you feel. She's alive right now because of you. We'll figure this out, and we'll help you find her, but not until we have all the information we need to make our next strategic move. And then, I'll take you back to the human world myself."

"Spoken like a true prince of Iskalt." Gulliver lifted his head and managed a hesitant smile for his friend.

. . .

"Toby? Toby!" A familiar shriek echoed down the hall.

"Brace yourself, Toby. Here she comes." Gulliver moved out of the way.

Toby winced, leaning back on a settee in the royal residence, where Alona had been fussing over him since the healers finally left him alone for the day.

"Toby?" Another frantic shout reverberated down the hall.

"Someone tell her to stop shouting." Toby clutched his head. "I can hear just fine now."

Gulliver opened the door to the sitting room, and Tia came stumbling in, still calling for her brother.

Toby threw his hands up to stall her. "I'll be fine if you stop shrieking like a lunatic. You're killing my head."

"Are you okay?" Tia dropped to her knees beside him. "Griff said you collapsed when you came through your portal."

"I'm fine. I just got a little too close to the explosions and hurt my ears."

"Can you hear me?" She raised her voice, smoothing a hand over his bandages.

"No need to shout." Toby winced again.

"Give him some space, Tia." Gulliver tugged her back to her feet, and she turned her attention to him.

"Are you okay?"

"Everyone's fine." Gulliver wrapped his arms around her, and his tail stroked her shoulder.

"Gul." She threw her arms around him. "I'm so sorry for sending Sophie back to that awful place. I thought it was the right thing to do."

"It's okay. I'll find her just as soon as I get back there."

"We have much to discuss first." Now that she knew

Gulliver and Toby were fine, Tia fell back into her role as queen in the span of a breath.

"Are you sure you're okay?" She sat down beside her brother.

"Really, I'm fine. I promise." He draped an arm around her.

"Good." She punched his arm.

"Ow! What was that for?" He rubbed his shoulder where she'd hit him.

"You brought an entire village of people through a giant portal, and you didn't send a single person off course? You all ended up exactly where you meant to go? It's not fair!" She smacked him again.

"Fair?" Gulliver snorted. "I think it's only fair that you aren't good at everything, Tia."

"But I'm *really* bad at it."

"It's endearing, sweetheart." Brea came into the room, making a beeline for her son.

"I'm fine, Mom." Toby let her fuss over him.

"I heard you passed out." She checked his bandages and studied his eyes. "You might have a concussion."

"I don't know what that is, but I just have a headache."

"He could barely hear for at least a day," Gulliver offered with a smirk when Toby shot him a glare.

"I heard" Tia shook her head.

"It got better. I'm fine now. Can we talk about something else? Like what we're going to do to help the half-fae camping outside of Radur City? And the ones still suffering in the human world?"

"We're going to meet with them soon," Tia said. "We will let them know they are welcome here now that they are finally home."

"That's just it, Tia." Toby shook his head. "They aren't home. You have to understand, they don't trust us. The human world is all most of them have ever known. To them, it's their home. A home they are willing to fight for."

"He's right." Gulliver moved to sit in a chair beside Toby. "They will never feel safe here. Most of them have very little magic, if any."

"Perhaps they will be more comfortable in Myrkur," Tia offered.

"I don't think we should force them," Brea said. "They're going to want to return to what is familiar to them."

"Are you suggesting we engage in an all-out war with the humans?" Tia's eyes widened in surprise.

"No, but we will have to do what's best for the half-fae."

"We just have to figure out what that is."

"I thought I might find you out here." Griffin jogged across the dusty Eldur road to catch up with Gulliver at the entrance to Aghadoon, just beyond the city.

"I have some people to check on." Gulliver shuffled his feet, waiting for his father to catch his breath.

"You wouldn't be trying to sneak back into the human world with a certain magic village now, would you?" Griffin tilted his head back to get a good look at his son.

"No, I don't know how to drive this thing." He let his hands fall to his sides. "But if you're offering a ride, I'll take it." They walked along the perimeter of the village where the half-fae had set up camp outside of Aghadoon. They didn't trust the village and preferred the tents Alona had provided them over the last remaining houses standing inside the walls.

"You've spent too much time in the human world." Griffin laid a hand on his shoulder as they walked. "You're starting to sound like Brea."

"Toby asked me to check on Xavier, and Xavier asked me to

check on Toby, so I'm going back and forth between them like a carrier pigeon delivering messages."

As they walked through the camp, Gulliver didn't miss the looks of scorn cast his way. Now that they were back in the five kingdoms, everyone could see Gulliver's dark fae features and they were either frightened of him or they didn't trust him.

"Here comes Xavier." Griffin nodded toward the tall young man headed their way. "I'll leave you to it. I have a meeting with Orla. She refuses to talk to the queens anymore, so I'm the envoy this time. Just don't tell her I'm technically a prince or she might refuse to talk to me too." Griffin patted Gulliver on the back and set off to find the scary warrior woman who led the half-fae camp.

Gulliver waited for Xavier to find his way through the crowd of very nervous-looking half-fae. He felt bad for them, stuck in a world they didn't understand. He knew what that was like from his time in Vondur. At least these fae had landed in a kingdom that would treat them right.

"How is he today?" Xavier's eyes were tight with worry. "I thought he was doing better, but he hasn't been down here yet."

"Toby's fine. He's just resting right now." Gulliver fell in step with Xavier, and they made their way through the haphazard camp. "His hearing wasn't great for a day or so, but it's better now."

"Sounds like a concussion. Do your doctors know how to treat such an injury?"

"They're taking good care of him. I promise."

"If he's so much better, why hasn't he visited yet? The people here trust him, and they are anxious to hear from a fae they've fought beside. Even if that fae has magic he lied about." Xavier's face clouded with anger.

Gulliver sighed, pausing to look around for a quiet place to talk. "Let's go sit in the shade." He pointed to a tall fire nut tree that had just begun to smolder. That meant the nuts were almost ripe.

"That thing looks like it's about to burst into flames at any moment," Xavier hesitated.

"It won't. And I'm ready for a snack." He rubbed his stomach and headed for the lone tree everyone else was avoiding.

"Won't it be hot over there?" Xavier reluctantly followed. "It's hotter than New Orleans in July, and that's saying something."

"Just don't touch the bark and you'll be fine." Gulliver sank down in the shade of the tree and gathered several smoking pods into a pile beside him. He searched his pocket for the carving knife he always kept with him and pried open a few of the pods for a snack.

"They grow ... toasted nuts here?" Xavier examined the contents of the pod.

"They're delicious, but they can cause really bad breath, so don't eat the unripe ones."

"I think I'll pass." Xavier set the large pod on the ground, and Gulliver shrugged, tossing several of the nuts into his mouth.

"He'll come when he's ready," Gulliver finally said.

"You mean when he's done hiding?" Xavier scowled.

"He doesn't have magic, Xavier. He never lied about that."

"I saw him open that portal. It was huge and ... so powerful." He dropped his head in his hands.

"And it's the only thing he can do. Well, that and he amplifies his sister's magic, but when it comes to what the fae here call magic, he is as powerless as I am."

"Neither of you are powerless. You have your defensive magic. What you two can do defies any magic I've ever seen."

Gulliver snorted. "Just trust me when I say what Toby and

I can do amounts to cheap party tricks compared to the five kingdoms—well, four kingdoms. Myrkurians are all like me."

"Then, why isn't he here?" Xavier's anger wilted until only sadness remained.

Gulliver looked up, gazing across the grassy plains to the desert in the distance, where the fire plains used to be. It was still hot in Eldur, but since the Vatlands failed and the land was reclaimed, the temperatures were changing. Eldur would always be a desert kingdom, but it was as though all the land was healing now. Green things grew where once there was nothing but hot sand and wiry bushes.

"Did he ever mention Logan to you?" Gulliver asked.

"No."

"I'm not surprised." Gulliver sliced into another smoking pod. "They were going to be married."

Xavier studied his hands. "I see."

"Logan was the Crown Prince of Eldur. He would have ruled here."

"Was? How did he die?"

"It was a terrible accident." Gulliver suddenly lost his appetite as he remembered the look on Logan's face when he fell after the molten hot lava struck his head. "It was less than a year ago." He dusted his hands clean and wiped the sticky residue from the pods on the grass. "Toby hasn't been back to Eldur since. He hasn't handled Logan's death. Like at all. Coming back here, seeing the people who would have been his family—seeing Darra and how much she looks like her brother —it's hard for him."

"I understand." Xavier nodded. "Can you please tell him I, um ... I miss him, but to take all the time he needs."

"Of course."

"Xavier! Get over here!"

Both men jerked their heads toward the commanding voice.

"Orla." Gulliver sighed at the look of frustration on Griffin's face as he jogged to catch up with her. "I'm guessing Dad's meeting with her didn't go well.

"Come sit in the shade, Orla," Xavier called.

"Not on your life," she shouted back. "I don't go near trees that look like that." She nodded at the smoke billowing up into the sky.

"They're supposed to smolder like that," Gulliver said.

"You aren't going to convince her." Xavier stood and dusted his jeans off. "Let's go see what she wants."

"What's happening?" Xavier asked as they crossed the distance between them.

"We have to go back." Orla crossed her arms over her chest. "And if these fae won't help us, we will find a way home on our own."

"We will help you," Griffin said, exasperated. "But you need to speak with Queen Tierney and Queen Alona."

"I don't talk to queens any more than I have to," Orla insisted. "You're an O'Shea. We know what that means." She fumed at Griffin. "We have some O'Sheas among us, you know. Their magic is strong, but not even they can open portals." She glared at him again. "So, if you please, make a portal and take us all home this instant."

"It doesn't work that way," Griffin growled at her. "First of all, it's daytime and my magic only works at night. Second of all, Toby is the only O'Shea who can make a portal powerful enough to carry you all back home at once. And right now, he's recovering from an injury. So, I'm afraid you're going to have to be patient."

"Fine. Bring Toby down to the camp as soon as he feels up to it."

"That's not going to solve the problem in the human realm," Gulliver interrupted their argument. "You're going to have to meet with the rulers at some point. You need our help, and they're the ones who are in a position to give it to you. We all want what's best for your fae."

"What if the queens and a few others come down to meet with you here in Aghadoon?" Griffin suggested.

"They can come to our camp," Orla relented. "But none of my fae are setting foot in that creepy city again."

Chapter Seven
SOPHIE

Nothing changed at the institute, making it hard to keep track of the days. Each morning, a gruff nurse woke Sophie to shove pills into her mouth. Then, she went through the day trying to appear like they affected everything she did. Dragging her feet in the halls, not speaking during meals, losing focus during the forced interrogation sessions they called therapy.

She knew what they wanted from her: the truth about everything she'd gone through. She held nothing back, knowing they would think she was lying to them, telling them a fantastical story that was too hard to believe of the creatures they hated so much.

A slamming door roused her from her half-asleep state. There was little true sleep to be had surrounded by the sterile white walls and antiseptic smell.

The man she'd come to know as Grantham stepped into her room, his large frame taking up so much space she could no longer see the door. He stared down at a tablet in his hand, not sparing a single glance for her.

"You're a lucky one today." He tapped something on the screen. "It's time to increase your meds. You'll be feeling really good soon." He finally lifted his eyes before turning to pull a cart into the room.

"You'll also start having twice daily sessions with Doctor Clarkson. He seems to think you could benefit from extra time with him." The nurse dumped pills from a tiny white cup into his hand.

Sophie couldn't see them, but she pictured them in her mind. A blue one. Two white ones. But an increase could mean anything.

He didn't wait for her to respond to him because she never did. Instead, he reached forward, gripping her jaw and yanking down. His other hand shoved the pills into her mouth and then handed her a paper cup with a few dribbles of water. "Swallow."

She did as she was told and then opened her mouth to show him it was empty, lifting her tongue, as was the routine. When he was satisfied, he gave her a single nod. "Door's unlocked today. Be careful where you go. We can see you. And don't be late for the doc."

The moment the door shut behind him, she ran her tongue up under her cheek to dislodge the pills and spit them into her palm. Lifting the corner of her mattress, she stashed them in an old Jell-O cup she'd tied to the bedframe.

With a sigh, she got out of bed. Her body ached, and her head pounded, but she couldn't stay in here all day. Not when she finally had a chance to figure out what was truly going on in this place.

If she hadn't imagined the boy entirely.

After talking to him in the dining hall, he seemed to have disappeared, as if he'd never been there at all. She tried not to worry, but now that the medications had worn off, her anxiety was at an all-time high.

Something wasn't right here. It wasn't simply a mental hospital.

Creeping out into the hall, she peered down the blank walls. A few patients moved slowly, aimlessly. Two nurses rushed past, but they paid her no mind. She wanted to yell at them that nurses were supposed to do no harm. With her illness, she'd known a lot of people in the medical industry, and they all had something in common. A deep desire to help their patients.

Here, something didn't add up.

"Library," someone whispered as they passed her in the hall.

Sophie turned to see the nurse who'd been so kind to her, the one the boy with no name trusted. It could have been a trap, but she didn't think so.

It took her asking for directions to the *library* to find the sad little metal cart half-filled with old books sitting at the back of the game room. Sophie thumbed through paperbacks, thinking there must be a note or something she was meant to find here. She lifted a copy of *Anne of Green Gables* and the cover fell off, landing at her feet.

Before she could reach for it, someone else was there, bending to retrieve the cover.

"They've seen better days." The boy looked up at her, those intense eyes holding secrets she wasn't sure he even understood.

"I don't think there's anything here that's been published in the last thirty years."

He carefully wrapped the bound book in its broken cover and placed it back on the shelf. 'I wouldn't know." He dropped his gaze and his toe grazed over a cracked patch of linoleum tile.

Sophie's eyes widened. If this boy truly grew up here ... "You ..."

He didn't know how to read.

Shame flickered across his face. "Sometimes, I take books back to my room and stare at the letters, imagining the stories they tell of the world outside. Is it beautiful?" He looked up at Sophie with eager eyes, thirsty for knowledge of a world he'd never experienced.

That wasn't an easy question. Yes, the world itself was a beautiful creation, but those living in it ... "It can be. Sometimes, living in the world means people helping one another with love and grace."

"And other times?"

She sighed, not wanting to take away the image he had of what lay beyond these walls. But he deserved honesty. "People are complicated."

It was the most universal truth. Her father, the man who killed her mother, also put her in here. Yet, she didn't want to believe it was his decision. Whatever he'd done, he loved her.

But did he love her more than he hated the fae? That was the hard question.

A hand slid into hers and squeezed. There was an odd comfort in the gesture. Despite them being strangers, it felt as though they were in this together, and always had been.

Sophie shook her head. That was a ridiculous notion. She'd only just met him, yet the little boy had already managed to steal her heart.

"Come with me," he whispered.

She didn't even need to nod. He seemed to know she wouldn't argue as he tugged her across the game room, where a few other patients sat dazed.

Out in the hall, he shoved her into a corner and peered up. Sophie followed his gaze to the cameras nearby as they oscillated.

"This is a dead spot," he whispered. "The camera can't see us. Doc doesn't want me talking to you. He says you have allied with the fae against humans, but—"

"I thought you said you didn't know what a fae was?" Sophie glanced around the corner to make sure no one could see them.

"I lied." He shrugged. "Too many listeners. The doctor doesn't know all I've seen. My earliest memories are of you, Sophie. I just didn't know your name, but I knew you would come for me eventually. I've been waiting for so long. This is the only life I know, but through you, I've seen so much more. I don't understand how, and I can't control it, but it has to mean something, right?"

Sophie didn't know what to say. "But I'm human." Even if he did have fae blood, that wouldn't explain why he saw her. Then, she remembered something he said before. "I disappeared from your dreams for a while. Why?"

He lifted one shoulder into a shrug. "One moment, you were in the hospital, and I thought for sure I was going to lose you. I was so inconsolable Doctor Clarkson locked me in my room for days. Then, you were gone. I thought you'd died until you suddenly showed up again and gave me hope."

None of it made any sense. Sophie leaned down closer to him. This kid sure knew how to tug on her heartstrings. "Why? Why do I give you hope?"

He paused. "Because ... this place is evil. If we're going to defeat it, we need each other."

"Back away." The shout came from farther down the hall. "Keep your distance." Two guards ran for them, black batons lifted in a clear warning. There had to be a reason for the odd and completely unnecessary malicious treatment of the patients here.

With no time to think about what she was doing, Sophie readied for a fight, putting herself in front of the boy. The first guard reached them and went for her, but his arm jerked and his body slammed into the wall, hanging there for a moment before he slid to the floor.

The second launched into the air, a scream echoing down the hall as he flew backward, landing in a heap.

"Sophie, run," the boy yelled.

She tried to reach for him, to help him keep up, but when she looked back, Grantham stepped in behind him and plunged a needle into his neck.

If Sophie didn't do something, she'd be next. She took off down the hall, slamming through the swinging doors that led to a row of offices where doctors provided their version of therapy. She'd never ventured past these offices, but there was a red door that basically screamed, "Open me!"

Footsteps sounded behind her and she went for the door, finding it locked. The heavy steel was immovable. It required a keycard to enter.

She only knew one person for sure who'd have one. If this door was so secure, there was something awful behind it. She had to know what it was.

Doctor Clarkson's office was near, and she peered inside, relieved to find it empty. His lab coat was draped over the back of the chair, as if he wasn't on duty today. But she knew differently. He was always here.

Making quick work of the coat, she rummaged through various pockets until she found a card clipped to the inside of the left pocket. Bingo.

"Ms. Devereaux." His sickening voice stopped her. "You're early."

Hiding the card behind her back, she tried to think of something, anything, to say to the man she detested. Footsteps sounded out in the hall, most likely the guards she'd run from before.

"I'll just come back, then."

"Not so fast, girl." He blocked the doorway.

There was no time for this. Sophie lunged for him, driving her knee up into his groin.

"Sorry," she yelled as he doubled over, and she sprinted past him. Hurting people wasn't in her nature. All she wanted was answers.

Reaching the red door, she fumbled with the key card until she managed to press it to the pad. The guards were almost on her when the door clicked, and she shoved it open, closing it before anyone could follow.

Her feet slowed to a stop as she took in the scene before her. Bright fluorescent lights flickered overhead, illuminating a hall not unlike the one she'd left. Except, this time, there weren't only doors lining the walls. There were windows looking in on people locked inside rooms like hers, though these patients were wearing restraints. Some lay on metal tables; others were forced to stand upright.

Window after window showed the horrors of the true

Clarkson Institute. The patients in her wing were a front, so the doctors could do whatever they did back here.

A symbol on the wall caught her eye, and she moved closer. It showed two ancient swords and four letters. HAFS.

This was a HAFS facility. She'd suspected it from the moment she saw Doctor Clarkson, but to see it so evident sent a shock through her system.

The people in those rooms...

Her question was answered when she was halfway down the hall. She stumbled back at the sight of a winged fae cowering under intense spotlights as someone in a white coat made notes on a tablet.

But ... how? She thought of Gulliver and the way his features weren't visible in the human realm. How had HAFS done it? They'd removed this dark fae's defensive magic.

The doctor or scientist or whatever they claimed to be jerked around, his eyes connecting with hers. There was no emotion there, only a grim determination. He stepped up to the window, still staring at her, and reached for a button on the wall.

Red lights flashed overhead as an alarm sounded. The winged fae met Sophie's eyes for a fraction of a second, but they were hazy and lifeless.

All she knew was she had to get out of here. She had to let both worlds know what was happening. Unable to go back the way she came, she ran for another door at the end of the ward, her legs tiring with each step. She kept going, despite the aches, despite the tears streaming down her face and the burning in her chest.

She'd grown up thinking the fae were evil, that they wanted to destroy humans.

Now, she knew the truth. There was nothing more evil than what she'd just witnessed in this human facility.

Before she reached the door, strong arms caught her from behind. Sophie bucked and kicked, trying to break free, but It was no use. Pain pinched her neck moments before her breathing slowed, and her body melted as she faded from the world.

Chapter Eight
TOBY

"Toby." Someone poked him in the side. Hard. It could only be one person. "Toby. Toby. Toby."

Groaning, he rolled over in the unfamiliar bed, thanking Alona once again that she'd thought to give him a room far from Logan's old quarters. "What do you want?"

"Your Majesty."

"What?"

"I'm your queen. The polite question would be, 'What can I do for you, your beautiful, smart, witty royal Majesty?'"

"Go away, your royal pain in the—"

"Hey!" Tia grabbed a pillow and smacked him upside the head.

Pain ricocheted through his skull, and he pressed a hand over his ear. "For magic's sake, T."

She sat back on her heels and bit her lip. "Sorry."

"You know, for a queen, you're quite annoying."

"For a queen, huh? Did you not see our own mother make it her life's mission to do things that made Dad growl like a wild animal?"

Toby couldn't help smiling. "I hear it every time I want to yell at someone."

"Brea Robinson Cahill O'Shea!" Tia imitated their father's voice. "What have you done now?" She fell beside him on the bed, her chest heaving with laughter.

Toby couldn't remember the last time he'd just sat with his sister and talked. It was probably before Logan died, before Toby gave up on himself and everyone around him. He'd started to believe they were all just waiting for the next tragedy, the next war. There was no escaping the constant cycle of conflict and strife.

Yet, there were also moments he wanted to believe in the good. Moments that seemed to disappear over the last year.

"I've missed you," Tia whispered. He knew she didn't just mean while he was in the human realm. Her hand found his among the cooling blankets. Eldur beds required a fabric that cooled one's skin while they slept to keep the heat from overwhelming them.

"You know I have to go back, right?" He refused to let the humans win this fight.

She sighed, snuggling closer. "Yeah, I figured. I want to go with you."

He didn't give her the permission she sought because it wouldn't matter. Tia would always do what she wanted. "You and me, side by side again?"

"Always." A breath pushed out of her. "Before you left for

New Orleans ... I thought I'd lost you. Physically, you were there, but mentally, the most important person in my life was a ghost."

He squeezed her hand, hating how he'd created the distance between them. "I'm trying, Tia. I promise you, I'm trying to be me."

"You don't have to be the same fae you were before, you know. No one is expecting that. We just ... we just don't want to lose you entirely."

"You won't. Being away from the five kingdoms, going to the human realm, and fighting for something I believe in again has reminded me of everything we've been through together. We've sacrificed a lot, but we've also done a lot of good."

There was a knock on the door, and it opened before Toby could say anything.

Gulliver stood in the doorway, staring at them with a frown on his face. "Not fair. I want to join." He bounded onto the bed like a spry fox and burrowed in next to Tia, wrapping an arm around her stomach. "This is how it's meant to be."

Toby couldn't argue with that. He, Tia, and Gulliver had a bond that was more powerful than almost anything he'd known. Yet, there was so much missing from the moment, so many fears hanging over them. He knew Gulliver thought of little else but Sophie stuck in the human realm.

She may very well have been welcomed back with open arms. Maybe she sat by and watched as they launched missiles toward Aghadoon. Her father was one of their leaders, after all. Toby wasn't quite as convinced as Gulliver that she was in trouble or that she was on the fae's side.

Then, there was the fact that the sacred fae village sat nearly destroyed outside Radur City. The half-fae didn't want to be here, and their kin were still in danger in the human realm.

"Tell me it's going to be okay," Toby said to both of them.

Gulliver reached out his arm so he was practically spread across both twins, and Tia rested her head on Toby's shoulder. Neither told him everything would work out, but they all knew they would have each other regardless.

Someone cleared a throat, and they all looked up to find Brea and Lochlan in the doorway. Lochlan only showed his amusement in the twitching of his brow. Brea, on the other hand, could never hide hers. She walked into the room slowly, her arms clasped behind her back. She looked impeccable, as always, with an ice-blue gown embedded with crystals. A grin lit up her entire face.

"Hate to break up the party."

His father grunted. "They're in bed, Brea. It's not a party, and you're not breaking anything."

Tia rolled her eyes. "It's a human expression, Dad."

Lochlan had never taken to the human speech, like every single one of his children had. His wife might have been fae, but she was raised in the human realm and it was deeply ingrained in her.

Gulliver rolled off them and sat up. Toby slid his legs over the side of the bed. "Is there a reason half the family is in my room this early in the morning? Is Griff or Kayleigh going to pop out of my wardrobe?"

"That would be fun." Tia shared a smile with their mother. There was something seriously wrong with the women in his family.

His father, seemingly of the same opinion, sighed. "A boy is in the courtyard asking for you."

Toby's entire body tensed before he forced himself to relax. He hoped his family didn't notice, but he was never that lucky. Tia rubbed his back, and his mother's lips turned down.

"He's a man, Loch. Not a boy. Stop thinking everyone

younger than you is a child." She patted his cheek. "This man says those you brought into Eldur wish to meet but will only do so in the camp that's been set up for them."

"Was that all?" Toby didn't know what he was hoping for. For Xavier to be so worried about Toby that he'd climb the terrace? For him to say they were ready to go back and fight?

His dad cleared his throat. He did that a lot. "He, uh ... has asked to speak with you."

Toby couldn't. Not yet. Not here. In Logan's palace, where they'd been so happy. Where they'd dreamed of a future amid the fountains and sandstone of Eldur. Logan would have ruled while Toby stood by his side, joining their families officially.

"I can't." His voice was barely audible, but everyone in the room heard.

"Toby." His mom's sad smile was enough to make him want to run.

He spoke louder this time. "I just can't."

His mom tried to speak again, but his dad put a hand on her arm to stop her. "Okay. We'll let him know." He practically dragged his wife from the room.

Toby slid from the bed on shaky legs. "I need to get dressed." His voice wasn't sharp, but it dismissed both Tia and Gulliver. Tia hesitated just like their mother had, but in the end, Gulliver was able to pull her away.

When the door finally shut, Toby leaned against the wall, breathing heavily. His empty stomach rumbled, but if he ate anything right now, he doubted he'd keep it down. Soon, a maid would arrive to prepare him a bath and help ready him to head to the great hall for the morning meal. He had to get out of here before they did.

Changing quickly, he pulled on a simple brown tunic and beige trousers that had been left for him. Once he laced up his boots, he marched into the hall, not knowing exactly where he was headed.

He needed to walk around, to find one of the many open-air courtyards to clear his head. There was one that contained a wishing fountain. Yes, that sounded good.

His feet had other plans because he soon found himself in a familiar part of the palace. None of the guards stopped him as he entered the royal family's residence. Darra was an early riser, so she was most likely already training. There were no wars to fight, yet she loved to start the day by sparring with her guards.

Finn normally inspected the guards and various parts of the palace early. Toby had seen it enough times to know the exact routine.

But Alona ... when he heard soft sobs coming from a familiar sitting room, he stopped, unsure if he should intrude. The door to Logan's suite of rooms was partially open, and he wondered if they looked the same. Did he still have a painting on the wall depicting him and his sister? Had the silvery blue rug been co-opted for another use?

He had to know.

Pushing the door open wider, the first thing he saw was Alona in the sitting room, perched on the edge of a cream-colored settee. She had her face buried in her hands.

As he made his way to the Eldurian queen, Toby vaguely noted that everything was just as Logan had left it. For most of his life, he'd called her Aunt Alona, despite there being no blood relation between them. She was an important part of his life. Yet, now, they stood on opposite sides of a chasm of grief, unable to help each other.

"Hi." He glanced down, suddenly regretting his intrusion.

Alona had never looked on him with anything but kindness, and that didn't change now. "Toby." She attempted a smile. "I haven't been in here since right after it happened."

"I heard you ... from the hall."

She patted the settee beside her. "Having you here has brought back memories." She wiped a handkerchief across her eyes. "All good memories, I promise."

He took the offered seat, not sure what to say. He went with, "I've tried to avoid feeling anything since it happened."

Her hand covered his. "That's not healthy, Toby. You should feel it all, feel it deeply. Logan is a part of your soul. If you cut him out, you lose a piece of yourself."

Tears gathered in his eyes. "For a while, I wasn't sure if I still existed without him."

"Of course you do." She smiled, the gesture small. "The man we both knew wouldn't want any of us to shut down. He was so selfless. All he'd want right now is for us to keep living our lives."

"I don't want to forget him."

She brushed a hand over his cheek. "Oh, honey, you won't. You have a big heart. It isn't supposed to remain broken forever." She paused. "I heard there was someone looking for you this morning. A human boy."

"He's half-fae."

She nodded. "Does this half-fae have a name?"

He sighed. "Xavier."

"Well, my little spy—"

"Gulliver, right?" He cursed. "That man can never keep his mouth shut."

"Not exactly." She wiped her eyes again. "From how I understand it, Gullie talked to Tia, who talked to Brea. Brea brought it to me that you spent a lot of time with this man in the human realm."

"He's a friend."

"One you care for a great deal. I can tell by the reddening of your cheeks. It's how ..." She drew in a deep breath. "It's how my Logan used to look when he talked about you."

Toby averted his eyes, unable to meet Alona' s gaze while she talked of Xavier.

"Do you love this man?"

Maybe he was wrong. His eyes snapped to hers. "What?"

"Those fae are terrified in this world that feels so strange to them. They won't come near the palace. Yet, he came."

"To deliver a message about a meeting spot."

She gave a watery laugh. "Griff had already brought that to us. Xavier braved the palace gates to see you. He even asked your father if he could speak with you, though I doubt he knew exactly who he was speaking to."

Toby could only imagine the look on Lochlan's face when that happened.

Alona squeezed his hand. "This man cares about you. You don't need my blessing to move on, to search for a new future, Toby, but just know that everyone who has ever loved Logan loves you too. All we want is for you to be happy. My son would want it too."

The weight Toby had been carrying in his heart didn't fall away, but he felt the cracks begin to form in the stone. Alona was right. He couldn't stay broken for the rest of his life.

I love you, Logan. He sent off the thought that would never really leave him. *But now I think there might be more to me than this grief.*

There had to be.

Chapter Nine
GULLIVER

Different place. Same meeting. The royals of the fae kingdoms fought about what was to be done as if they even had a say. Gulliver paced the length of the makeshift meeting room they'd created outside Aghadoon. It was open to the sky, with no real walls around it, only guards keeping all those who weren't invited away.

Alona shook her head, clutching the arms of her seat, one she'd had brought from the palace. "These human weapons ... you claim they aren't magic?"

Brea stomped her foot like she was trying not to throw scathing remarks her human sister's way. "Of course they're not. Is anything we ... they do magic?" She pushed a hand through her dark hair, lifting her eyes to the sky. "Relax, Brea. They're trying to understand."

"Is she talking to herself?" Xavier leaned close as Gulliver stopped moving.

"She does that."

Brea turned so quickly both men fell back. "Gulliver O'Shea, if you have something to say, let's hear it."

Her stare could have pierced the iciest lake.

"Mom." Tia laid a hand on her shoulder. "He didn't mean anything by it. I think you need a moment. Let's get some space."

Brea relaxed under her daughter's touch. "Fine."

The two women walked past the crowd of those who'd come to discuss the human war and ducked around the line of guards.

Gulliver let out a breath, and Toby clapped him on the back. "Don't worry, Gul. She's snapped at each of us over the last few days."

Unlike the rest of those who lived in the fae realm, Brea had connections to the humans that ran deep. She knew what they were capable of without seeing the destruction Gulliver witnessed. For most of her young life, she'd believed she was one of them, and those ties didn't just go away.

The only other resident of the five kingdoms who could possibly understand was conspicuously quiet. Myles sat on the ground in the grass at the back of the group.

Neeve cleared her throat. "So, are we saying we wish to act on behalf of our half-fae brethren?"

"Yes," Toby said at the same time his father said, "No."

They stared at each other, both stubborn enough to wait for the other to break.

Gulliver couldn't believe they didn't see it. The kings and queens he'd fought beside. The ones he knew would protect their world from any threat. They were the ones he revered, respected, loved. And yet, at this moment, they were so unbelievably obtuse.

"Stop," he yelled. They kept talking. He looked to his father helplessly.

Griff dipped his head. "This isn't about them, Gul. You've seen it, you've been there. For once, make them listen instead of lead."

Riona slid her hand into his. "Royals are the most stubborn fae."

"She doesn't mean me." Griff winked.

Gulliver almost laughed when his mother rolled her eyes and said, "I definitely mean him. In my experience, you have to be loud. And repeat yourself. A lot."

Loud. He could do that.

Gulliver drew himself up to his full height. His tail lifted, ready for anything.

"Stop talking!" The words came out as a high-pitched screech. He hadn't meant to sound like one of his sisters when they heard the word no, but there it was.

The group fell silent, all eyes turning to him in surprise. *Great job, Gullie. Now you're in for it.*

Brea and Tia chose that exact moment to return, stopping nearby.

"What's wrong?" Tia was alert, on edge.

Alona folded her hands in her lap and said calmly, "It appears Gulliver wishes for us all to shut our mouths."

His face warmed, and he was sure it was as bright as a ripe Gelsi berry. "I didn't say that exactly. I just ..."

Tia bit back a smile, clearly enjoying this a little too much. "You just what, Gul?"

"My father says I need to make you stop trying to lead so

you'll listen." He suddenly didn't know what else to say. His tail dipped and wrapped around his middle.

Brea bumped her shoulder against Griff's. "He would say that, but making any of these guys listen isn't exactly a piece of cake."

Every full-blooded fae in the room stared at her like she'd sprouted two heads.

Lochlan sighed. "I never know what it means when she suddenly starts talking about cake."

"Brea." Alona looked at her with concern. "If you're hungry, I can call for something, but I doubt we have cake at this time of day."

Gulliver ground his teeth together. The human world was burning, destroying the places the half-fae humans called home, and they wanted to speak of cake? "Can we focus?"

Alona's face sobered. "Yes, of course. You had something you wished to say, Gulliver. Go ahead."

Finn gave him an encouraging nod from his place next to his wife.

"Respectfully, none of you understand the kind of damage these humans can do. Some of their weapons fly."

"So do some of ours." Riona's wings flicked in agitation.

"Yes, but Mom, you can't blast holes through Aghadoon's protective shields in mere seconds as you fly over."

Silence followed his words before Lochlan spoke. "The shield was up when that damage occurred?"

Brandon had kept silent until now. He stepped forward. "Yes. Their ... bombs ... ripped holes in the shields, shattering the ancient magic that has protected the village for as long as it has existed. And it happened faster than any of you can imagine. Griffin and I attempted to hold the shields in place with our own magic, but it was far beyond our capabilities. We had no choice but to escape the human realm altogether. If we hadn't, Aghadoon would be nothing now but ruins for the humans to pick over. And much of our magic would be destroyed forever."

"Can we not defeat them with magic?" Kier asked. He was still new to having an unlimited amount of magic now that he could use as many fire opals as he wanted. To him, it could solve almost anything.

Gulliver shook his head. "Have any of you been listening?" He couldn't believe it was even a question. "This group, the Human Alliance for Survival, developed because of their fear of us. Survival. It's what they want. They believe we are going to enter their world and destroy everything they love to take it for ourselves."

He'd only strengthened that belief when he'd stolen the daughter of one of their leaders. Yet, no one knew where Sophie even was.

"But we don't want their world," Neeve said. "We just can't allow them to terrorize our fae who choose to live there." She ran a weary hand over her brow. "It would all be a lot easier if they'd all just come home and leave the human realm to the humans."

Gulliver sucked in a gulp of air. "All our half-fae friends want is the freedom to live their lives in their own homes, without the constant fear of discovery. Yet, you all sit here discussing how we're going to go about doing exactly what the humans expect us to do. Destroying them with a power they couldn't begin to understand."

Lochlan's brow creased. "If we cannot go to war with the humans to save the half-fae, then how are we to defeat them?"

"We don't. It's time we listen and we help however we can." Toby met Xavier's gaze, and Xavier nodded, encouraging him to continue. "It's not our fight. We need to help them, but we cannot take control. Alona, Neeve, Tia, Hector, Bronagh, our half-fae friends are not your subjects. We are simply their allies, nothing more. Why don't you let them lead us in this?" He stepped aside, letting them all see Orla clearly. "Orla, why don't you take it from here."

To her credit, she didn't hesitate to come forward. "The first thing you must understand is that HAFS does not represent all humans. They have the support of certain governments, but there are plenty of people who do not fear us."

Brea offered her a smile. "Thank you for that. It's good to remember that our war is not with the humans but with this specific group."

Orla didn't return the smile before she continued. "We know a lot about them. We have the names of their leaders, the government officials who've authorized bombings. We know the people they have inside our society. Their job is to alert HAFS to upcoming threats. They know you can travel between the worlds. There's even a way they've created to determine where you have entered the human realm. It appears the atmospheric pressure changes after a portal has been opened."

"A thinning of the veil," Brandon said. "That's what we call it."

Orla nodded. "They're tracking your movements."

Griff cursed. "That means none of our normal destinations are safe."

Tia and Brea shared a look.

Orla went on. "HAFS is dangerous because of their dedication, but also the strict punishments they enforce on their own members. It's created a culture of parents turning in their own children as suspected changelings. Wives and husbands accuse each other of fae heritage."

That was ... horrible. Gulliver couldn't imagine ever turning on someone he loved. His mother squeezed his hand, probably thinking the same thing. They'd both grown up in a place where fae did just that, where they turned on each other for scraps of food and the promise of living another day.

"There's a place ..." Xavier hesitated, his eyes flicking to Brea for a moment, as if he knew something he wasn't saying. "A center where the children suspected of fae blood are sent. We have one person on the inside, but it's locked down so tightly it's nearly impossible to communicate with her. All the employees of the institute are tracked, watched.

"It's headed by the worldwide leader of HAFS, his pet project. We don't know exactly what happens there, but we do know many of the kids sent are guilty of nothing more than misbehavior."

Gulliver looked from Xavier to Brea as her face went pale. A place for children suspected of magic ... Could it ...

"This man," Brea choked out. "What is his name?"

"Clarkson. Doctor Alec Clarkson."

She shook her head, stumbling into Lochlan. He held her up. "Clar ..." She couldn't get his full name out.

It was Griff who said what those who knew Brea's story must have been thinking. "The Clarkson Institute is a part of HAFS?"

"But we only learned about them recently." Tia's eyes didn't leave her mother, worry swimming in their depths.

"There's a story among the half-fae," Xavier's voice wavered, "of a fae child raised in the human realm and being sent to Clarkson. Many of us in the half-fae movement now are young. So many of our elders were killed over the years of fighting them. We were not around when it happened, but we know it like we know our own life stories. The Clarkson Institute was the stuff of our childhood nightmares, run by the doctor's father before him. We do not know when he started HAFS, but it has been around for a very long time."

Brea shrank in on herself. Gulliver didn't know everything

she'd gone through at the institute, only that it was not a place he'd wish on his enemies.

His thoughts stuttered as he realized how much Xavier and Orla knew that they'd never told him. All Brea had to do to be sent to the Clarkson Institute time and again was exhibit tiny bits of power, to see features on people others claimed not to see, and her parents themselves handed her over.

Would another parent do the same?

He caught Tia's attention, and realization entered her gaze. Without looking at Xavier, he asked, "And what would happen to a dying woman who returned healed?"

Xavier's face went through a range of emotion, finally settling on dread. "I suppose they'd do whatever they could to find out what happened to her."

"Even if she's on their side? Even if her father is one of their leaders?" He already knew the answer to his own question.

"Especially then."

Chapter Ten
SOPHIE

Sophie. The name rang in her head, but she barely heard it beyond the pain splitting her skull. *Sophie.*

She groaned, unable to grasp a thought, to hold on to it. Her head was foggy, her limbs heavy. She pried her eyes open only to find her vision swimming before her.

She was back in her room, but this time, nothing was the same. Her entire body felt like it was wedged under a massive anvil, unable to move.

Clear your mind, Sophie.

"Wha..." She tried to speak, but her tongue stuck to the roof of her mouth.

It was a long shot. I can talk to you in my dreams, but I never should have thought it was real.

"Real?" she whispered. "Real ... it's real!" Her eyes darted around the room, looking for the source of the voice. "Where are you?" She moistened her cracked lips and pushed herself up so she was sitting. "Hello?" The words slurred coming out, but she couldn't speak any clearer.

Whoa! It's you. Sophie, can you really hear me?

"Uh, huh." She recognized the voice now. The boy she'd barely gotten to talk to the day before when they drugged her and ... images flashed through her mind. Fae, glamours removed, strapped to metal beds. Winged fae surrounded by humans in lab coats.

Slow down, the boy said. *Don't speak out loud, I'm only in your head. But think all of that again so I can catch it.*

She didn't want to. It was horrific, but she did as he asked, squeezing her eyes tightly shut.

She could almost feel him quiver, and chills raced down her spine. What was this? How was it possible?

I don't know, he answered a question she hadn't asked.

But... I'm not really fae. I don't have this kind of magic. Was it because of the water in the healing pools?

No, I've always seen you. I guess it's different now since you can hear me in your head, but maybe it's because you know of my existence now.

Why us? What are we to each other?

Another thing I've never known. You're just the girl in my dreams, and now I'm the boy in your head.

Maybe she did deserve to be here. She really was going crazy, losing her mind.

No one deserves to be here. The voice in her head quieted, replaced by images that flashed before her eyes like a movie.

A little boy sitting on his own in the dining hall, begging for something more to eat. That same boy, slightly older, tied to those metal beds she'd seen before. What had they done to him?

You've been here your entire life.

My earliest memories are of this place.

She got a flash of sadness and fear from a child who should have only ever experienced love. The only light she saw in his memories was fluorescent. No sunlight, no silver shine from the stars.

You've never... Her thoughts stuttered as tears flooded her vision. This boy had never been outside these walls. He'd never looked to the moon or made a wish on a shining star, felt a warm breeze rifling through his hair.

Don't cry for me. The words were no more than a whisper in her mind.

It was more than words and images she felt. A power buzzed along her skin, making her hairs stand on end. The only time she'd felt anything like it was... *You're fae.*

I'm not sure.

Yet, his dreams were real. He could speak in her mind. This wasn't a power she'd gleaned from the healing pools. It was his.

Did they know?

She tried to swing her legs over the side of the bed, but they didn't budge. Strong fabric straps looped around her ankles, where metal buckles pressed painfully into her skin, keeping her secured to the bed. She'd been too numb to notice.

What's wrong? the boy asked, probably sensing her distress.

My legs. I can't move. She reached for the buckles, but it was no use. Her fumbling fingers and foggy mind couldn't figure them out.

They do that sometimes. The nurses will come take them off eventually. He seemed so resigned to this life, but what had he said the night before?

You knew. She leaned back on her elbows as the realization hit her. *You said this place was evil. Did you know about the fae kept in chains?*

I've only seen fae in my head, so I don't know if I'd recognize one, but those rooms, yes. They use them for study. The group that runs this place—

HAFS.

Whatever they call themselves they don't have good intentions.

You said we could beat them together. How?

She even heard his sigh. *I said we had to try.*

Something about this boy, about his power called to her. He was important. She just didn't know how or why.

The doorknob to her room turned, and she threw herself back, closing her eyes. The boy faded from her mind and she breathed a sigh of relief. She was afraid someone might look at her and realize she had a giant secret.

When Grantham entered, he went through his routine of pouring pills into her hand, and she dutifully sat up and shoved them in her mouth. At least this time he didn't do it himself with his grubby hand.

Hiding the pills in her cheek, she opened for him.

He didn't say a word as he nodded and pushed the cart from the room, shutting and locking the door behind him.

She spit the pills into her hand, wondering if this was a cycle she'd suffer for the rest of her life.

Maybe Gullie shouldn't have saved her. Surely the death that should have been hers was better than this.

Another day at the institute. Another day she had to figure

a way out. She refused to die in this place. Cancer hadn't taken her, neither would hate and fear.

First, she had to know what was happening, had to help the fae stuck in those rooms with the dark windows.

There was more security here than ever, armed guards stationed at every door. It wouldn't be as easy as last time to get to them, but there was another way.

Don't do it. The boy's voice in her mind was the only thing keeping her grounded some days. He wanted to protect her, even though he was just a kid, but this was for him as much as for her. Something inside of her needed to help him, to get him to Gullie.

Gulliver would know what to do. She had more faith in him than she'd ever had in anyone, and she still wasn't sure why.

Two guards had their hands on her arms as they marched her toward Doctor Clarkson's office. She dragged her feet, stumbling here and there like the walk troubled her, like the drugs kept her from fully rousing herself.

Clarkson's office had military medals framed and hanging on the walls. Now, he led a group the U.S. government once considered terrorists—before they joined them.

A guard pushed Sophie down onto the couch before they left her alone, waiting for the doctor. She knew they wouldn't be far, but the space was a luxury she couldn't get used to. It allowed her to breathe, to truly consider what it was she had to do.

A few minutes later, Doctor Clarkson breezed into the room in a rustle of lab coats and heavy boots. He was young, maybe in his forties. His father started the institute, but he died many years ago. Sophie remembered her dad talking about the two Clarkson men he had to answer to. He obeyed them, listened to them.

Now, she was here because he had to prove his loyalty to them.

Doctor Alec Clarkson sat at his desk, not saying a word as he leaned back in his leather chair.

Sophie refused to look away from him, not this time. She kept her eyelids heavy, so it appeared the drugs hadn't worn off, but she studied him. The way he breathed slowly, silently, his chest barely moving at all. He sat with complete stillness, a predator waiting to strike. His eyes were bright, almost kind. An illusion.

He steepled his fingers on his desk and leaned forward. "We've had quite a struggle with you, Sophie-Ann."

She wanted to tell him not to call her that, not to say her name at all. Instead, she gave him a drooping smile. "I..." She coughed. "I'm sorry. My curiosity got the better of me."

He pressed his lips together, watching her as if he could see right into her soul. "And that curiosity... was it satisfied?"

"Oh, yes. You're doing God's work here, Doctor. My father would love to see all you've accomplished. If you'd let me call him—"

"That is not possible." He pushed his chair back and stood, rounding the desk to stop in front of her. "I want us to understand each other. HAFS is only trying to protect our people. Do you understand why you're here?"

She nodded so hard it sent pain stabbing through one eye. "When the fae abducted me, I knew returning would be hard." The word *abducted* felt like a betrayal of Gullie. It was exactly what he'd done, but now, she couldn't hate him for it. He'd saved her, and she would never be able to thank him properly, to tell him that she was wrong. About everything.

Doctor Clarkson sat next to her on the couch like they were old friends and she wasn't a prisoner he kept drugged. He put a hand on her knee, and it took everything in her not to shy away in disgust. "We need to know what they did to you."

Until now, she'd fought. She'd done everything she could to keep them from believing the truth, but maybe a different truth was more important.

She let tears well in her eyes as she thought of Gulliver and never seeing him again. "It was awful." She sniffed. "The magic they used...."

His hand tightened on her knee. "An abomination."

Now was the part where she had to give up the little freedom she had left. "I think it's still inside me. That's why I'm alive. Do we even know anything about them, really? C-can they turn us into fae?" She let her voice tremble, but she wanted to laugh at the idea. Fae weren't mythical vampires.

Clarkson nodded like she'd exposed one of his fears. "We are studying them. Learning everything we can. What you saw in those rooms ... it is us protecting our fellow humans from a future controlled by the fae and their magic. Knowledge is our greatest weapon. We've been studying them for decades right here."

She bit back a grimace and forced a smile. "Thank the Lord." Her hand found his forearm and squeezed. "I know now that you're saving us. I've been a part of the alliance my entire life. Now, I might be one of them. How can I still help HAFS if I'm the very thing they hate?" She only had to plant the idea, knowing it would grow in his mind.

He stood and started pacing in front of her. "There's a way, but I hate to subject one of our own to that sort of treatment."

She rose to her feet, facing him. "Anything. Doctor Clarkson, I want to help the cause. No matter what happened to me in the fae realm, no matter what I may be now, I will still do whatever is necessary for my people."

He gripped each of her shoulders, looking down into her

eyes. He didn't seem to notice how she no longer swayed, that the haze of drugs didn't cloud her irises. Instead, he smiled. "Sophie-Ann Devereaux, your father would be proud of you."

Those words, that one sentence, once would have bolstered her. Now, they did nothing but enrage the fire already burning in her heart.

Chapter Eleven
GULLIVER

Gulliver gripped the hilt of the sword strapped around his waist, trying to make himself remember why it might be a bad idea to draw it on his best friend.

"Tia, you're the newly crowned Queen of Iskalt. You cannot leave for a jaunt through the human realm when it isn't necessary," Brea argued with her daughter.

Tia stomped her foot. "Dad did it all the time!"

"Your father never left this realm during the first few years of his reign. It's important for your people to see you're devoted to them while you establish your rule."

"That's crap. They'd never even know I left." Tia's eyes

flashed with annoyance, and Gulliver took a step away from the warring mother and daughter.

"You have a lot to learn if you think servants don't talk." Brea folded her arms across her chest. "You're not going and that's final."

"That might have worked when I was ten and not the Queen of Iskalt, Mother, but I'm an adult and I am going to help Gulliver."

Gulliver cleared his throat and prayed he'd get through to them quickly before they wasted any more time. "I don't care who comes with me, but we need to leave now. Dad," he turned to his father, "can you open a portal for us? These two can figure out who's going to follow, but I'm leaving."

"And I'm coming with you," Tia insisted.

"We're wasting time, Brea." Griffin shared a look with the former queen, his eyes pleading with her to speed this along.

"Sophie needs me." Gulliver's hands clenched into fists at his side.

"You're right," Brea relented. "Let's go, but Tia can't be gone long before people begin to talk."

"Keir will keep them happy." Tia rolled her eyes. "He can return to Iskalt to make sure the place is still standing. They like him better than me anyway."

"Not true," Brea said in a soothing tone. "They adore you, darling. Always have."

"Maybe, but my husband is better at this job. He'll cover for me."

"I'll do what now?" Keir asked as he entered Alona's study with a pile of documents that likely needed Tia's attention.

Gulliver heaved an annoyed sigh. "We're going after Sophie, and Tia's coming. You have to take care of Iskalt while we're gone, which we're doing right now." He marched through the open doors into the walled garden that overlooked Radur city.

"What he said." Tia paused to give her husband a peck on the cheek before she followed Gulliver into the garden.

"We'll be back soon." Brea tucked a pair of daggers into the belt at her waist. "If you need anything, Lochlan is with the children in the village. He'll take you back to Iskalt tonight. Er ... don't tell him if you don't have to."

"Um, okay." Keir clutched the huge stack of papers to his chest and watched in confusion as Griffin opened a portal in the moonlight. "Have fun ... I guess." He waved from the doorway as Gulliver stepped through his father's portal into the human realm yet again.

"Can't we just call a human to come get us?" Gulliver paced across the living room at the farmhouse. "We did that all the time in New Orleans."

"I'm not sure we can get an Uber out here in the middle of nowhere." Brea tapped her fingertips across the screen on the phone she kept here.

"How are we going to get to the institute?" Tia paced in the opposite direction of Gulliver, throwing her hands up in the air. "This is why we need a car."

"None of us know how to drive, Tia." Brea's thumbs flew across the screen. "I never learned."

"How did you grow up in the human realm and not learn to drive?" Gulliver asked.

"I was only Seventeen when I left, and my parents never taught me. There wasn't time with all the work we had to do around the farm and my stays at the institute. Plus, they weren't exactly parents of the year."

"Did you get in touch with Mrs. Merrick?" Griffin asked.

"That's what I'm doing now if you all will hush up and let me text."

"What's wrong with dropping by to ask for a lift? We could have walked over to the Merrick farm by now." Gulliver groaned impatiently. They'd been there for hours now, waiting for the day to wane. The sun was sitting low on the horizon, and he was desperate to find out if Clarkson had indeed taken Sophie to the institute where Brea had spent so much time as a child. He couldn't fathom what they might do to her in a place like that. He didn't like the grim look Brea wore whenever she recalled her time there.

"It's rude, and humans are accustomed to texting," Brea murmured. "She's going to come pick us up and give us a ride into the city. I've told her it's not safe for her to stick around, so we will have to find our own way back."

"Hopefully it'll be through a portal with Sophie safely with us." Gulliver picked up his pacing. "When will she be here?"

"She's on her way now. Let's get a few things straight before she gets here. We have to blend in as best we can, so we need to change into human clothes. Keep your weapons concealed, and just ... don't act like a fae."

"Nice, Mom." Tia rolled her eyes. "How do you propose we do that?"

"Just do your best." Brea sighed and went upstairs to change into her preferred jeans and t-shirt attire. "And keep your ears hidden."

With Gulliver's defensive magic, he appeared human when he was in the human realm, and he knew how to dress. He went up to Toby's room and raided the closet for jeans that were a bit too short and a t-shirt that read "If I was a JEDI, there's a hundred percent chance I'd use the force inappropriately." He didn't know what a JEDI was, but the shirt fit. He didn't care too much about hiding his sword either. Getting to Sophie was more important than keeping the humans from suspecting he was fae. As Brea had said many times before, all a human had to do was have a conversation with Gulliver to know he wasn't from earth.

Once they were finally in Mrs. Merrick's giant car speeding along toward the institute, Gulliver was able to relax. All they had to do now was figure out a way in and then back out. Easy, right?

"Good luck on your mission!" Mrs. Merrick called as she drove away. After so many years of dealing with the fae family her son had married into, she never seemed phased by their antics. The drive into Columbus took longer than Gulliver would have liked, and it was nearly dark now as they walked along the sidewalk a few blocks from their destination.

"Can you two at least try to blend in?" Brea hissed at Griffin and Tia, who were calling too much attention to themselves with their behavior on the busy street. Griffin walked too close to the curb and Tia kept falling behind, staring up at the tall buildings like a tourist seeing a big city for the first time.

"For magic's sake, you act as though you've never seen a city before," Gulliver said, urging them all to keep up. "We're not here to sight see, Tia."

"Sorry, Gul, it's just been so long since my last visit." Tia skipped along the sidewalk to catch up to her mother. "I forgot how wonderful it is here, but why are there so many cars on this little street? Are they all going to the Clarkson Institute?"

"It's rush hour, honey," Brea said. "People are just going home. I need you to act normal and keep up."

"I am normal," Tia insisted.

"Grown adult humans don't run around like hyper squirrels on vacation in a city like Columbus. Especially this close to a mental hospital."

"Gullie, move your sword to your right side and try to keep

it hidden so people can't see the glint in their headlights." Brea ignored her daughter.

"Can we just hurry?" Gullie moved his sword so the hilt faced away from the fast-moving traffic.

"Griff, they won't honk at you if you stay away from the curb. And don't raise your fist!" Brea shouted, shaking her head. "Fracking fae idiots. I've a mind to leave you all at the institute for a little therapy."

"We're nearly there." Gulliver pointed across the street to the heavy stone facade of the Clarkson Institute. "We just need to find a way in through the back." He kept walking past the institute, studying the layout with the security guards posted at the entrance to the parking lot.

"I forget how to get across the street when the cars refuse to stop." Tia's eyes widened at the flow of so many cars. "It's like a raging river without a bridge."

"We use the crosswalk, Tia." Gulliver pointed to the intersection ahead. "Seriously, how long has it been since you visited a human city?"

"A few years." She sniffed irritably. "And New York has the yellow cars that take you where you want to go so you don't have to walk so much."

"Hush, both of you." Brea pulled Griffin in close as the four of them approached the crosswalk, and Gulliver pressed the button. "Thank heaven at least one of you has learned something in your time here." She gave Gulliver an appreciative nod.

"Hey, I've learned lots of stuff." Griffin sounded affronted. "I know how elevators work now, and I've actually ridden a streetcar successfully too."

"Let's just get out of this busy intersection." Brea guided them across the street like a group of nervous ducklings following their mother. "We'll take the side street and see if we can find an alley entrance somewhere that's not guarded."

Gulliver and Brea hurried down the quiet street and away from the traffic. Griffin and Tia followed, leaving the cacophony of blaring horns and loud music behind.

They stayed on the opposite side of the street from the institute, looking for a way in that wouldn't call too much attention to them.

"Look for a loading dock," Griffin whisper-shouted. "That's how we got into the hospital in New Orleans."

"Until we got kicked out," Gulliver reminded him.

"Let's not get caught this time."

"Let's," Brea said nervously. "It will not go well for us if we're caught inside the institute. It's not like a hospital."

"I thought this was a hospital." Tia rushed to keep up. Dressed in her human clothes, she no longer looked like a queen. She looked more like his best friend than she had in months.

"It is, but it's not the type where the patients can come and go as they please. It's similar to a prison."

"We're breaking into a prison?" Griffin slowed his pace. "Is that the best plan?"

"It's the only plan." Gulliver darted across the street and ducked into an alley between the main building of the Clarkson Institute and a second darker, more menacing-looking structure tucked behind it. An enclosed bridge seemed to connect the two buildings. A long span of dark windows greeted them, and no sight of a single guard anywhere.

"Over here, Gullie!" Tia called to him in the darkness. The way the buildings were situated, a hush had fallen over them, sending the noises of the city into the distance. It was as though they had entered another world. One the humans didn't see sitting among them.

This was where bad things happened to good people. Gullie could feel it in his bones.

"Don't touch that door!" Brea hissed, rushing to her daughter's side.

"But it says it's an emergency door, and I think this counts as an emergency." Tia pointed at the big red stripe across the door, marking it as an exit only.

"It will set off an alarm if you try to go through it." Brea pulled Tia away from the door. "We need to avoid alarms."

Gulliver glanced around the shadowed alley, where weeds grew up around smelly dumpsters. "Why are humans always so gross?"

He studied the windows around the doors. They were narrow and long, and the glass looked thick, but there was already a crack. And where there was a crack, there was weakness. Gulliver raised the hilt of his sword and ignored Brea's shout of, "No!"

It took several attempts, but he shoved his way through the glass, creating an opening just big enough for him to slip through.

"Careful!" Tia cautioned him, but Gullie managed to get through without seriously injuring himself on the jagged glass. "Open the door for us."

Gulliver reached for the door just as a loud beeping sounded, making him flinch.

"Um ... Hide!" Brea shouted, dragging Tia and Griffin away from the opening.

"Mom, we have to help Gullie," Tia protested. "We have to help him save his girl."

"I think we're going to have to let him save his girl on his own."

A pang of fear shot through Gulliver as he realized Brea was right.

The beeping grew louder as he searched his surroundings. He was in a large storage room with plenty of places to hide. Ducking behind a crate of small boxes containing white gloves, he just managed to avoid being seen when a bright light burst overhead and a man in all white clothes peeked into the room from another door.

"What's going on in here?" he demanded, rushing into the room to discover the broken glass. "What in the— Someone's escaping!"

"Well, now we have to run." Gulliver just made out Brea's irritated tone.

While the man was busy searching for the escaped patient, Gulliver tiptoed around him and shot through the open door into a maze of small, sad offices with short walls and claustrophobic proportions.

"Hey, you, come back here." The man lumbered after him.

Gulliver reached for the nearest door and tumbled into a bright white hallway, gloriously empty.

He almost lost his pursuer when he reached another hall filled with dark windows displaying dark fae trapped behind the white walls of the institute.

"Stop!" The man lunged for Gulliver, grabbing his arm. "Escapee!" he shrieked, but Gulliver brought down the hilt of his sword on the man's head to shut him up.

Chapter Twelve
TOBY

"Absolutely not." Orla stood at the head of the table in the library of Aghadoon. Her gaze sparked with anger as she met Queen Alona's incredulous stare. It took some convincing, but they'd finally gotten her into the village.

Toby shifted slowly to step between them, uneasy with the tension in the room between his father, the Queen of Eldur, and the leader of the L.A. fae community. His father only just returned from a quick overnight trip to Iskalt five minutes ago and looked exhausted.

"Whyever not?" Alona asked. "This is your home. Of

course, you are all welcome here in the five kingdoms, wherever you wish to settle."

The look on Xavier's face told Toby exactly what most of the half-fae would think of the queen's offer. Kind though it was, it would not be accepted.

"And we appreciate that, your Majesty, but with all due respect, this is not our home." Orla glowered at her. "It has never been our home. You should know how that feels more than anyone else at this table."

"How so?" The Eldurian queen tilted her head in question.

"Are you not human?" Orla asked. "Can you imagine if some monarch from the human realm decided your place was among their own subjects simply because you are one of them? To have a perfect stranger decide this world was not your home?"

"I see," Alona murmured. "Yet, I do not live among a people who wish me dead simply because I am not like them. My life here is not one of strife and heartache. Would your fae not have a much better life living among others like them?"

"Alona," Toby interjected, "the half-fae do not have the powerful magic of this world. What magic they do have is frightening to the humans, but we are frightening to them. They view themselves as humans in a strange land they do not understand. A land that lacks the technology and conveniences they are accustomed to. We cannot keep them here against their will when we only brought them here in a dire moment that left us with little choice. They want to go home, and I believe it is our responsibility to send them back and do our part to help them find peace within a world they understand."

"We have to think of our own fae, son," Lochlan said. "We can't risk a war with the humans, and if we interfere, it will likely come to that. We need to consider all our options, and what might be best for the half-fae communities is to bring them all here where they can be safe."

"I agree with Loch," Alona said. "I think it's important that every member of your community feels welcome here," she addressed Orla. "They need to know their futures could be here among their own kind should they choose to stay."

Orla shook her head and slammed her fist against the table. "No. We are not like you, your Majesties. You are all so eager to embrace our fae sides and welcome us to your lands, but you forget we are more human than fae. And that makes the human realm our home. Thank you for the kind welcome and assistance we desperately needed, but we must forge our own path."

Toby moved to stand beside Orla. The fierce warrior woman was scary, but he could see the pride she held for her people. Pride and determination to do right by them.

"Maybe my son is right." Lochlan sighed, looking like he wanted this conversation to be over so he could find his bed. "And he is wise. Orla represents her people just as you represent the people of Eldur, Alona. She knows what is best for them."

"Thank you, your Majesty." Orla nodded in Lochlan's direction. "My people here in the village are scared and eager to return to their homes and their families. There are countless fae back home facing HAFS on their own. To even think of bringing them all here is foolish. There are too many. Too many families that have been separated. Some don't know where their loved ones have gone. It is for them that I fight." She laid a palm gently on the table, as if to erase an unseen mark her fist left in her earlier frustration.

"Then, I think it is clear what we need to do." Toby's voice rose with confidence. He was prepared to fight alongside Orla.

Even if that went against his parents' wishes. It was time to stop talking and start acting.

"Which is?" Alona asked.

"We will offer our half-fae friends refuge here for as long as they need it, but we will actively help them get back home as safely as possible. But we will not abandon them. We will help them find peace with the humans."

"I agree with Prince Tobias," Lochlan said, a hint of pride in his voice.

"I need to return to the human realm as soon as possible," Orla said. "My people need me there. Those who wish to stay behind will be safe here under the supervision of one of my trusted soldiers. Until arrangements can be made to bring them safely home."

"At moonrise tonight, I will take you back myself," Toby offered. "I would caution you not to take everyone home at once. With a few, we can slip into L.A. unnoticed. And over time, my father and uncle and I will help transport everyone little by little."

"Of course, if that is what you want, then that is what we will do." Alona fussed with the hem of her gauzy sleeve, clearly not happy with the direction this meeting had taken. "But how do we negotiate a peace treaty with the humans when their first reaction is to come at us with explosions and ... so much hate?" Her eyes filled with a sadness and uncertainty Toby was all too familiar with.

"*We* might not be able to avoid a war with HAFS." Toby shared a look with Xavier. "And we may very well have to make a show of power against the true enemy to display our might. To show the leaders of HAFS they have no hope of defeating our collective magic. But the fae of the Five Kingdoms cannot lead that fight."

"That is not our way." Alona shook her head stubbornly.

"We have had peace for so many years now. None of us want to return to the days of fighting and division we knew when we were your age, Tobias. I will not have another war on our hands."

"Then, let it rest in my hands. And in the hands of other leaders like me," Orla said softly. "We are prepared to fight. I just ask that you do not hinder us from doing what is right for our people. Our enemy is HAFS, not all of humankind. There are many who will support us. Young Toby has taken the first steps to create a real home for us in Los Angeles. A place where we can live openly and at peace alongside those humans who do not fear us."

"Perhaps it is best for the five kingdoms to take a step back from this conflict," Lochlan suggested. "Orla is right; it is not our fight."

"But there are fae who have been needlessly traumatized in this conflict," Alona argued. "I can't sit back and let that happen when there is so much Eldur can offer."

"Eldur can support our cause without fighting for us." Orla stood back with her arms clasped behind her like a soldier. "We do not need an army or weapons. We can and will fight our own battles. We just need ... friends, allies to cheer us on and help us show the humans they have nothing to fear from us as long as they stop the persecution against us. Friends who can provide refuge, if and when it is needed ... should it come to that."

"I think we can all agree that Orla's requests are perfectly reasonable and the very least we can do is aid her and her people," Finn spoke up for the first time, drawing a glare from his wife. "And the rest can't be decided this instant anyway."

"Very well," Alona relented.

They all knew it wouldn't be the end of the conversation, but it was a start.

Chapter Thirteen
SOPHIE

Leather straps bound Sophie to the cot, and all she could think was, at least it wasn't the metal tables she'd seen the others on. A rough blanket scratched her skin, and it felt like ants crawled beneath the surface.

She squirmed, but it was no use. There wasn't a way out now.

I chose this. The thought popped into her head so suddenly it surprised her, but it wasn't wrong. She put herself here, subjecting herself to whatever Doctor Clarkson and the others planned for her. And she did it to help them, the fae she once hated.

They didn't kill my mother. For so much of her life, she'd thought their power was evil because it took the kindest, warmest mother from her. Even now, she could picture her mother's smile, the way it dimmed when her father neared.

How had she never seen it?

Where are you? The boy's voice had been gone from her mind since the first morning it came to her, yet now it felt as familiar as anything. A comfort in this dark place.

I don't know, she responded, not wanting to tell him the truth of what she'd done.

Yes, you do.

She'd forgotten he could see her in his dreams. There was no lying to the kid with no name, the one who had never felt the sun on his skin yet was more intelligent than most people she knew.

Doctor Clarkson is going to try to find out what the fae did to me.

The boy didn't respond at first, but her anxiety rose, almost like he was projecting it into her head.

Whatever you did, it was a mistake.

Sophie closed her eyes, shutting out the irritating fluorescents. *I didn't have a choice.*

I know.

She knew he did. Unlike the rest of the world, he saw how truly evil this place was. That the fae weren't the enemy. Instead, the enemy was among her own people.

She pictured Gullie with his unique feline eyes, the way they seemed to see all the way to the bits of herself she tried to keep hidden. He'd have done the same as her, risked himself to fight for what he believed in. She might never see him again, but she desperately wanted to prove him right.

Others may have questioned the faith he had in her, but it

didn't waver. He'd seen something before she even saw it in herself, a reason to risk the wrath of his queen. He knew she was better than HAFS, that it wasn't her destiny.

Who is that guy? the boy asked.

She stopped struggling against the straps and let her breathing calm. Who was he? To his fae, Gullie was just a friend of the queen. To her father, he was the fae who abducted her. And yet ...

The fae who saved me. Not only her life. He saved her from herself. *And the one who is going to find us.*

I hope you're right. His uncertainty simmered across the bond.

Sophie smiled, despite her predicament. It was her turn to have faith. *I am.*

The door opening jerked her from the conversation, from the thoughts that almost made her forget what was coming.

Doctor Clarkson walked in, his heavy steps echoing the sudden pounding in her head. It felt like fists striking the wall she'd erected in a single moment, a wall to keep others out.

The boy.

She had to prevent him from knowing what came next.

"Miss Devereaux, I am sorry for the restraints."

"If you're sorry," she bit out, "then release them."

He gave her a sad smile. "I'm afraid they are necessary. You agreed that we must know if the fae infected you, if their magic has changed you in a dangerous way."

Tears stung the corners of her eyes. "What are you going to do to me?"

"Only what we must."

He gestured toward what looked like a mirror. She knew it wasn't what it seemed. From that hallway, others could look in and observe what was done.

The pain in her skull intensified, but she didn't know how to lower the wall and let the kid back in, even if she wanted to. "Please don't hurt me."

The door opened again, and two others walked in wearing white coats. Between them, they pushed a large device that stood on two wheeled legs. The top of it looked like an array of solar panels, but she'd seen what this could do.

Clarkson put a hand on her arm. "Your father wanted me to tell you how proud he is. Once we are finished, you may be able to return to him."

How could she possibly go back to the man who killed her mother? The same man who would hunt down Gulliver the first chance he got. She forced a smile. "I do so wish to do right by him. He's done so much."

Clarkson looked satisfied with her answer. "Sophie, let me introduce you to Doctor Clara March. Our breakthrough device is her invention. And Doctor Nathanial Kline here is a recent hire of ours. He wishes to study the molecular makeup of our fae foes in order to determine where exactly their magic originates."

It didn't make sense, this studying of the fae. HAFS' goal was to protect human life, ensure the survival of all peoples. So, why study the fae? Why break them down and learn of their magic?

Unless ...

It couldn't be real. The followers of HAFS, the governments involved, would never approve of it.

Doctor Clarkson wished to replicate magic without a fae host. Was it possible he wanted to bring their power to the human race?

Her tears dried as she saw the man before her in an entirely new light. It was genius. Convince generations of humans to turn on those suspected of having magic while his father and now he would study and learn and prepare.

The rage that surged through her came with none of the magic he suspected her of having. It was purely human instinct. She had to get free, to warn ... someone. She wasn't even sure who'd listen to her.

Gulliver.

He wouldn't even question it. If he didn't find her, she had to get to him somehow.

Doctor Kline approached with a needle in one hand. It was connected to a long rubber tube that stopped at an empty bag. "I just need some blood."

He was asking her permission while the restraints kept her in place. It was such an odd circumstance. A laugh burst out of her.

"Take it." She turned her arm to expose a vein in the crook of her elbow. "All of it if you like. I don't care."

Doctor Clarkson frowned. "Nathanial, bring me the Fentanyl."

Sophie kept calm, despite the urge to rip each of her captor's hearts right from their chests. She was well versed in the various pain medications from her treatments, but Fentanyl was the worst of them.

Clarkson approached with a syringe. A small needle protruded from the end. "Nothing to worry about. It will relieve some of the pain and keep you calm."

"No!" She tried to yank away from him. "I don't want it. Stop." No more drugs, no more remaining calm. She screamed, the sound piercing the barrier inside her mind, crumbling it to dust. Stars swam before her vision.

Sophie! The boy yelled in her head. *What's happening?*

"No. No!" She thrashed, but it was no use. The needle

pierced her arm, and the plunger descended, pushing the poison into her veins.

Her protests weakened as the doctors watched, waiting for what, she didn't know. It only took a few minutes for the drowsiness to come. Her limbs grew heavy, immovable.

"I'm going to take some marrow." She heard Doctor Kline's voice, but it sounded far away. Somewhere else.

There was pressure on her skin, the feeling of it splitting, and then a sharp pain as a needle went into her bone. Not even the medication could take that away.

Tears fell down her cheeks, and she couldn't wipe them away.

Someone wrapped a bandage around her leg while another moved the device into place above her. It rattled as Doctor March adjusted it, tilting it so one of the solar panel-like sides pointed directly down at her.

Her head swam, and the boy never stopped talking.

What are they doing to you?

Tell me what's going on.

Sophie, please.

She couldn't respond, couldn't formulate the thoughts necessary to explain any of this. Her eyelids sank as they grew heavier.

The first sound from the machine was a low hum. All three doctors filed out of the room, but she knew they wouldn't go far. They'd watch and wait. If they didn't want to be near the device, what did it do to those without magic?

The hum intensified, vibrating through every cell in her body.

Her chest jerked as if pulled by some magnetic source, arching off the cot. Her wrists and ankles struggled against the restraints.

That lasted for what felt like hours before a blast of light erupted from the panels, slamming her back onto the bed.

A scream tore from her throat as the ache turned to pain searing down her legs. It drew every bit of calm from her until her body writhed and bucked under the agony.

"Please," she cried. "It's too much." In all her years of cancer, she'd never experienced such pain. The device drained the life from her, pulling it straight from her heart.

Is this how it removed a fae's glamour? Revealed their magic? Fat tears bridged over her nose, dropping from the end as sweat dotted her brow. She didn't have any magic to pull out of her, nothing to protect her. Yet, they wouldn't stop until she did.

Doctor Clarkson didn't believe she'd come back healed and human. That much was clear.

It's killing you, the boy yelled, tears in his voice. *Fight, Sophie. Don't stop.*

I can't, she pushed the thought to him, but she didn't know if it got there.

Her blood felt like it was boiling, building up with rage and desperation and ... something else, something unfamiliar. Except, not entirely. She'd felt it once before.

The light of the device was suddenly less intense, the pain fading away with the heat racing along her skin.

She drew the light into her body, absorbed it like a sponge, cleaning up someone else's problem. It entered every cell, finding those that were healed in Lenya.

Maybe Doctor Clarkson was right.

She hadn't come back the same.

A smile curved her lips as power that didn't belong to her curled in her gut, waiting for its moment to break free. The leather straps burned where they touched her skin, reducing them to ash.

The device sparked and sputtered, the metal frame bending. Her eyes found the mirror. On the other side were the ones responsible for every evil this place perpetrated.

A place was only as bad as the humans that controlled it.

Light burst from her every pore, filling the room with the power of the device built to reveal the fae.

Keep going! the boy yelled.

She didn't understand how his power fueled her now, but now wasn't the time to ask questions. It was time to run.

Sparks rained down on her as lightbulbs burst, spraying glass across the room.

The door opened, revealing two guards with rifles. She jumped from the cot and lifted a hand. The barrels of their guns bent upward, and they flew back into the cinderblock wall, sliding down, unconscious.

The three doctors scrambled from the room in a panic. For once, they were the scared ones. Alarms blared overhead, and a red light flashed. Soon, the hall would be awash in guards. She had to find the boy and get out of here.

There was no time to deal with these three.

"You're ..." Doctor Clarkson choked.

Sophie stopped moving, looking into his eyes. "Human."

She was still human, that much she was sure of, but she'd have time to figure it all out later.

She'd just turned away when there was a thump behind her. When she looked over her shoulder, Doctor Clarkson was slumped on the ground with a man standing over him wielding a sword.

"I used the hilt," Gulliver said. "I didn't kill him."

Doctor Clarkson's blood trickled from a gash in his head, but Sophie didn't help him.

"You're here." Her eyes met Gulliver's.

"I'm—"

She didn't wait for him to finish, stepping over the doctor's body while the other two cowered against the wall.

"You're here," she repeated, pulling Gulliver to her. When she fit her lips to his, a breath of surprise escaped him before he returned her kiss as if he'd come to an institute that tortured his kind just for this moment.

Chapter Fourteen
SOPHIE

"Run, Gullie! Don't wait for me." Sophie clutched the hospital gown they'd forced her into for these experiments and struggled to keep up with Gulliver's long strides. Her stomach heaved at the way the world whirled around her, but she stumbled forward, hoping adrenaline would kick in and chase the effects of the Fentanyl from her body.

The boy's power had given her strength for a brief moment, but it was gone now.

"I'm not leaving you. Now, how do we get out of here?" Gulliver slowed the gurney they'd thrown the unconscious Doctor Clarkson on. They neared the end of the long, dark hall, and it was up to Sophie to figure out which direction to go. It was only a matter of time before the orderlies came at them with more drugs. And then, she really would be useless. They had to get out of the institute and fast, but Sophie couldn't leave the boy.

"I don't know." She glanced behind to the armed guards pursuing them and darted past Gulliver, checking a series of wide double doors until she found one that was unlocked. It opened into another hallway just like all the others. "Let's just keep running until I see something I recognize."

"Are you okay, Sophie?" Gulliver heaved his shoulder into the gurney to get it moving again, and then they were through the doors. Sophie slammed the lock in place, leaving the guards to find another way around. "What did they do to you?"

She rushed ahead, searching for anything that looked familiar. Her vision blurred, and she was certain she was slurring her words, but she had to keep moving. She had to clear her head or they were going to find themselves in even worse trouble now that they had threatened Doctor Clarkson.

"You don't want to know what they're trying to do here, Gul." Sophie ran frantically, looking for signs that would lead them back to the halls of the patient ward. From there, she should be able to find a way out. After she located the boy.

"This way." She helped Gulliver navigate a turn in the corridor that spilled them out into a wide space lined with windows and what seemed like miles of linoleum floors. The floor sloped up in an incline that connected the building they just left with the part of the institute Sophie was most familiar with.

"I think I know where we're heading." She picked up her pace as they struggled to push the gurney up the ramp. For the moment, they'd lost the armed guards, but they had minutes at best.

The orderlies here were bad enough, but she didn't want to mess with the guards and their automatic weapons. If they got their hands on Gulliver, she shuddered to think of what their machines might do to him and his defensive magic.

"Whatever happens, Gullie, you can't let them take you." Sophie sucked in a breath. Her head swam and her legs didn't want to cooperate. "If you have to leave me to save yourself, promise me you will."

"No." Gulliver shook his head furiously. "I'm not leaving without you."

"I don't want you to get hurt because of me." Tears choked Sophie's throat, but she kept pushing the gurney, her legs like lead weighing her down. The drugs made her movements slow and her thoughts foggy.

As they reached the top of the incline, they pushed through double doors into the main institute.

Sirens suddenly blared overhead, and flashing red lights illuminated the dark hallway with an otherworldly glow. She could hear patients crying and shouting as they reacted to the disturbing alarms. They'd stumbled into the fae ward.

"How about let's not get caught? I like that plan better." Gulliver grabbed her hand and pulled her along, shoving the gurney ahead of them as they picked up their pace again.

"Should we just leave him behind?" Sophie panted. "He's slowing us down."

"We're going to need the doctor for negotiations." Gulliver slammed the gurney into another set of double doors, and they burst into a hallway Sophie recognized. It was the one with the one-way windows.

"Oh, Gullie, don't look." She didn't want him to see what Clarkson was doing to others like him.

"I've already seen it." They charged past an unconscious

orderly lying in an open doorway. "I hit that guy on the head with my sword too."

Sophie glanced down to see the blade in question sheathed at his narrow waist. Something hummed in her chest at the idea of Gulliver wielding it. She remembered him sparring with it, imagined he was better than she knew considering his father was a fae prince who was probably a master swordsman himself.

Her cheeks flushed at the thoughts rushing through her mind about the combination of Gulliver's tall, lanky physique and his adorable geeky vibe, coupled with his fae warrior side she didn't know as well. She liked the contradictory combination, but now was not the time to get caught up in such distractions. Shaking her head, she pushed those thoughts aside.

"We should let the other fae out." Gulliver slowed to a stop and rummaged through the doctor's pockets for his keys.

"Yes." Sophie grabbed the keys from Gulliver's hand and moved to unlock the nearest door, her hands trembling.

A young woman with skin that shimmered like fish scales in a thousand beautiful colors greeted her with a hiss of hatred.

"Help the others." Sophie tossed the keys at her. "And get them out of here!" She didn't have time to wait for them all to escape, but it was the best she could do for the Dark Fae the doctor had been experimenting on for who knew how long.

"What are they doing to the Dark Fae here?" Gulliver glanced back as they raced down the hallway, leaving chaos behind them as dozens of angry fae poured out of the rooms.

"We can thank the good doctor for destroying the one thing keeping them safe in this world. He's managed to strip them of their defensive magic, Gullie." Sophie panted. "That's why you cannot let them take you."

Gullie nodded. "The Asrai back there can definitely take care of herself, but if she's been out of water a long time, she'll be weak and a bit addled. You don't want to run into an Asrai having a bad day."

"When we get out of this, you'll have to tell me what an Asrai is." Sophie skidded to a halt at intersecting hallways. "Through there!" She pointed at a door marked with room numbers.

"We need an exit, Sophie." Gulliver turned in a circle. "Look, there's a red sign down that way."

"No," Sophie shouted. "I can't leave without him."

"Who?"

"There's a boy with no name. He's been helping me, and I won't leave him behind."

Something cracked in Gulliver's expression, and for some reason it gutted her, seeing such a hurt look cross his features.

"Okay." He nodded without questioning. "Let's go find your friend."

"Get in here!" The nurse with the pretty eyes opened the door to the patient wing, waving them through as though she'd been waiting for them. The boy clutched her hand as they rolled the doctor through the doorway.

"See, I told you she'd come find me." The boy tugged on the nurse's hand.

Bedlam had erupted in the ward, and terrified patients ran up and down the halls, shouting and screaming along with the wailing sirens. Orderlies chased them down, ignoring Sophie and Gulliver and the nurse who probably just saved their lives.

"Oh, you really meant a little boy." Gulliver beamed a huge smile at Sophie when she took the boy's hand.

"I'm not little. I'm ten. At least, I think I am."

"He's been helping me." Sophie was relieved to see him again. She crouched down beside him. "Are you hurt?" She checked him over.

"No, but they hurt you." He pressed his palms against her

cheeks, his eyes filled with a shadow of pain she realized he'd probably experienced right along with her.

"I'll be okay," she assured him. "And I won't let them hurt you anymore."

"You three need to go," the nurse said as she waved her key card in front of a keypad that opened the double doors to a small empty waiting room. "Take this." She thrust the card into Sophie's hands. "It'll get you through the next two doors and into the staff parking lot. You can take my car." She shoved her keys into Sophie's hands. "Just do not get caught. You have to get out of the city. These are HAFS soldiers, and they will not stop. They practically worship him." She gestured at Clarkson. "They'd do anything for him."

"Why are you helping us?" Gulliver asked, a look of confusion in his face. "I thought all humans hated us."

The nurse shook her head. "Not all of us. My grandmother was half-fae, and HAFS killed her for it. They'd kill me if they knew I had even a drop of fae blood. It's time we all work together to stop this kind of hatred." She lifted the little boy onto the gurney at Clarkson's feet. "Keep him safe."

She turned back to the patient ward as HAFS guards flooded in from all sides. "Run!" She shut the double doors behind her as gunfire erupted.

"No!" Sophie screamed as blood splattered across the narrow windows. The nurse slid to the floor and more gunfire exploded. Tears streaming down her cheeks, she reached for a tall lamp in the corner of the small waiting room, Sophie ripped off the lampshade and dashed the bulb against the floor before she shoved the slim metal rod through the door handles to slow anyone pursuing them.

"Let's get out of here, Sophie." The little boy pointed to the metal door with the big red exit sign labeled 'Employee Exit Only'.

Sophie swiped the dead nurse's card at the keypad, and they moved into another long hallway. Only one more door stood between them and freedom.

Two HAFS guards managed to get through the barrier and chased them down the hall.

"No!" Gulliver shoved Sophie toward the door and drew his sword. He leaped up onto the gurney, putting himself in front of the little boy with no name. "Take one more step, and he's dead." Gulliver flicked the sword point at Clarkson's neck, drawing a thin line of blood.

"Drop your guns on the floor," Sophie shouted, fumbling with the key card.

"You heard the lady." Gulliver pressed the blade harder against the doctor's throat. "Drop your weapons."

"You don't have the guts, you filthy fae abomination," one of the guards taunted Gulliver, refusing to lower his weapon.

"I have guts just like a human." Gulliver crouched over the doctor. "And what would it matter if I didn't? Would that make me any less of a person?"

"You're not human. That makes you filth." The first guard took a shot, but Gulliver ducked.

"Don't you dare shoot that gun at him," Sophie shrieked, wishing she had something to throw at them.

"Drop the sword, boy, before you hurt yourself."

Gulliver smiled. "You should know, I'm not afraid to use this sword. I've been training all my life, and it wouldn't be the first time I've had to fight against evil. I've seen the things your doctor has done to my people. All the worlds would be better off without him in it. Even yours."

"Come on, kid, this is over. I won't hesitate to shoot you." The other guard lifted his gun.

"No!" Sophie shouted, but she needn't have. Her jaw dropped as Gulliver leapt from the gurney, swinging his sword.

Blood splattered as his blade found purchase, and the guards screamed. Gulliver drove them back down the hallway, relieving them of their weapons until they disappeared behind another door, bleeding from their wounds.

"Gullie?" Sophie's voice came out breathless as he marched toward her, shoving his sword back in its sheath. He didn't have a scratch on him. She hurried down the hall to grab one of the guns and slung it over her shoulder.

"You have that door open yet, Soph? I'd really like to leave this place now." Gulliver grinned, his cheeks flushed with pleasure at whatever expression he found on her face.

Sophie shoved the door open and headed across the parking lot. "Let's get out of here."

She smiled back at Gulliver and the three of them—and the unconscious Doctor Clarkson—rushed out into the night.

Chapter Fifteen
GULLIVER

Gulliver would rather face a host of guards with his sword than a stone field of human automobiles. He stood too stunned to move as he scanned them in the night. It was like entering a jungle with no knowledge of what kind of creatures lay in wait.

"Which one do you think is hers?" Sophie fumbled with the keys until she gripped a tiny black box between her fingers.

"What is this place?" the boy asked, his eyes just as wide as Gulliver's.

"What?" Sophie didn't look at him as she scanned the rows. "A parking lot. Have you never ..." She stopped speaking, and Gulliver wasn't sure why.

He'd seen parking lots in New Orleans, but one never got used to giant metal structures that could move without magic.

A beeping sound came from one of the automobiles as lights flashed.

Gulliver fought the urge the shriek and jump into Sophie's arms. "What's happening? Have they found us?"

Even in the dark, he could sense she rolled her eyes as she started walking. "No. That nurse just has good taste in cars."

She approached the sleek red car that shone in the nearby streetlight that appeared to take power directly from the moon. Where else would it come from in the middle of a parking lot?

Sophie yanked open the door before looking at both Gulliver and the boy. "Are you two coming, or would you prefer to go back to the institute?"

Both boys scrambled to lift the unconscious Doctor Clarkson into the car and then climbed in after him. As the engine rumbled, Gulliver couldn't get the image of the half-fae nurse out of his mind. He'd seen enough human weapons by now to know what they were capable of, but it was still shocking every time. How could they be scared of magic when they were so much more powerful?

Well, at least more powerful than most fae. He really wanted to see Tia and Brea take them down...

Oh crap!

"Wait!" Gulliver yelled as Sophie sped through the parking lot.

She slammed on the brakes, and they lurched forward. Gulliver's head smacked the dashboard, and he groaned. "What'd you do that for?"

"You don't yell at someone when they're driving. I thought you saw something with your fae vision that I was going to hit."

The boy leaned between the seats. "You're fae?"

"I don't have better vision just because my eyes look different. You were driving just fine. A little fast for my taste, but we're almost out."

She gripped the wheel tightly. "Then, why on earth did you yell at me?"

"Oh, that. Um ..." He rubbed his throbbing forehead. "I kind of forgot I didn't come here alone."

"How do you forget that?" Her voice rose an octave, one step away from panic.

"I saw you and ..." He shrugged. "Tia and Griff are going to kill me."

"You brought a queen and a prince to the institute and just left them?" She pressed her foot down on the gas, and the car jolted forward. "Guess we're going back in."

"Two queens. And last I saw them, they were near the side entrance. I got in that way." He pointed down a narrow street behind the building.

Sophie was quick to turn down the street. "We'll never find them this way."

She parked and jumped from the car.

Gulliver scrambled out after her. "We'll find them. She's not even your queen. Why are you so worried?"

She turned so fast he almost slammed into her. "Because they came for me. Me, a nobody. Someone whose own father wrote her off. The last person who truly cared for me died many years ago. Yet, they're risking capture to free me."

His brow creased. He didn't understand. "But ... that's what we do. We care about each other more than our own lives."

He couldn't fathom a place where that wasn't the case, where people thought of themselves before their loved ones.

Tears glistened in her dark eyes, reflecting the starlight. "We have to find them."

"We will. Come on." He took her hand and turned back

briefly. "Boy. Keep an eye on the doctor. If he wakes, make sure it isn't for long." He pulled a dagger from his hip and slipped it into the boy's hands.

"We'll be right back," Sophie said. "I promise."

Gulliver knew nothing of the kid Sophie insisted on saving, nor any of her reasons, but he trusted her. More than he'd thought possible of any human.

The boy looked scared, but he nodded and watched them run off into the darkness.

Noises danced through the night, a high-pitched song. He slowed to hear it.

"Police sirens," Sophie explained. "We don't have much time."

They sprinted along the side of the building, looking at every possible entry point, but there was no sign of them. Had they been caught?

Was it really a mistake bringing the Queen of Iskalt here?

Guards poured from the side entrance into the night, running off in pairs to search their surroundings.

Gulliver pressed Sophie up against the side of the building to avoid them. His breath came heavily as two armed guards rushed by.

He could feel Sophie's every movement, her intake of air. Her chest rose against his and wide eyes lifted. Her lashes dipped down, brushing against her pale cheeks, and he couldn't move, couldn't breathe.

Just standing was a struggle.

His entire body was on fire, delicious flames licking up his spine. "Sophie," he whispered.

She placed a hand on his chest, and for a moment, he thought she'd draw him closer, that she wanted to repeat the kiss neither of them had acknowledged. Instead, she pushed him back. "They're gone."

Air rushed into his lungs. "Are you sure?"

She nodded, tucking a strand of blue-tinted hair behind one ear. "But I don't think Tia or your father are out here."

A curse escaped him. "They must have made it inside already. We can't leave without them."

"I know."

Her words held so much meaning, and he realized she did know. She felt it too. Even with her human blood, they were hers. Her people. The ones who came for her.

"Come on." He led her back toward the front, where they'd seen the guards, and drew his sword. If he had to fight his way to Tia, Griff, and Brea, he would.

Three patients ran out the door and down the steps before the guards stopped them, aiming their guns right for their chests. Gulliver had to do something. He had to help them. When the human police got there to reinforce the guards, there'd be no hope.

"Stay here," he muttered, hoping Sophie listened to him.

Yet, when he walked forward, he could sense her steps behind him.

The guard at the front turned and started yelling, his long gun aimed at Gulliver.

"Stop right there!"

Gulliver kept going. This would be so much easier if he had Tia's power.

"I said stop." There was fear in the man's voice, but with so many tortured fae now running loose, Gulliver didn't blame him.

"I'm not going to hurt you."

Bullets pierced the night, coming from three guards at once. Gulliver lunged back to cover Sophie. Something fast sailed right past his head and he sucked in a breath as he stood from his crouch.

"Well, now, I can't keep my promise." It was something Tia would have said, and he needed to channel her anger to protect Sophie. Releasing her, he whirled to face the guards before they could shoot again. The blade of his sword cut through the first like he was made of air.

The second stumbled back, but Gulliver wasted no time jumping toward him. Lessons with his father, sparring with Tia and Toby, it all came back to him now.

The third guard took off running, but Gulliver didn't chase him. He looked to the patients who were frozen in place and jerked his head toward the street. "Go."

He didn't have to tell them a second time.

"That ..." Sophie couldn't get another word out as her entire body shook.

He sheathed his sword and drew her close. "We really need to get out of here."

Heat radiated off her, and her shaking slowly calmed as her pulse beat against him.

Yelling came from the direction of the car, and they looked at each other before they took off running. Gulliver didn't know anything about the boy other than that he was a child and couldn't protect himself.

Except, he was wrong.

Sophie skidded to a halt, and Gulliver crashed into her before taking in what she saw.

"You can't have him," the boy yelled.

"Kid." It was Griff. "Hand over Doctor Clarkson, and we'll let you go on your way."

"No!" Power radiated from him, striking Griff in the chest and tossing him into the air. He sailed in an arc before slamming into the ground next to Gulliver.

Griff groaned.

"Nice of you to finally show up, Dad." Gulliver had no

trouble admitting how entertaining this was, even if they didn't have time for it.

The boy let loose another bit of magic, but Brea blocked it.

Tia stormed toward Gulliver. "Where have you been?" She stopped. "Oh, Sophie. Hello. I'm glad you're not dead."

"Ringing endorsement." Sophie smiled.

"I don't know what that means." Gulliver had long since stopped asking. "But we need to go. Oy! Boy!"

The boy had a hand lifted toward Griff again. "About time you came back. These ones want the doctor."

"As much as I enjoy watching my father sail through the air, we have to go." He walked toward the car and put a hand on the boy's shoulder. "He's with us. Everyone, get in." The sirens grew louder as they piled into the car. There was no time to open a portal and get through, so it was the best they could do.

Except, when Gulliver looked at the back seat, Sophie sat smashed against the door.

"No." That meant ...

Tia slammed her foot down, and they sped through the dark city streets, whirring past cars with red flashing lights on top.

"Slow down," Griff yelled.

"Not likely." Tia sped up, and Gulliver gripped the door handle so tightly he was sure his knuckles turned white.

"Watch out!" he screamed as the side of the car scraped against another, busting off the oddly shaped looking glass in the process. Tia veered away from an oncoming car, a grin spreading across her face.

"Mom, we need these in our world."

Brea looked as green as Gulliver felt. "Not on your life, kid."

Sophie was mumbling something, but Gulliver couldn't hear her. "What?"

She didn't meet his eyes. "I'm praying."

Doctor Clarkson made a low sound, but he didn't get a chance to make another before the boy hit him on the head with the hilt of Gullie's knife, making him go still again.

There was more to this kid than met the eye. The magic, the willingness to do what it took.

Gullie would need to learn more about him if they survived this car ride.

By the time they reached the farmhouse, the car reeked of Griff's puke. Gulliver practically fell out of the door, his throat hoarse from yelling.

"I just want to go home." Brea dropped to her knees in the grass. "Where there are no cars my daughter can drive."

"Want me to open a portal?" Tia, the only one who didn't look disturbed by that ride, asked.

"*No*!" Gulliver, Griff, and Brea all yelled.

"Yeesh." She crossed her arms. "You get your friends lost in a hidden kingdom one time, and everyone suddenly thinks you can't do magic."

"Griff." Brea pushed to her feet. "Please do it before our queen here gets any ideas."

It wasn't until Griff opened the portal and Gulliver stepped through that he realized he'd done it.

Gulliver O'Shea saved the girl.

Chapter Sixteen

TOBY

"Can we be done with portals for a little while?" Sophie clutched her middle, like she was going to be sick. Toby was familiar with the feeling. Whenever he went through someone else's portal, it was a nauseating experience. He prided himself on the smooth transition of his own portals. The one magical thing he could do better than anyone else. The one magical thing he could do, period.

"Rough landing?" He offered her a hesitant smile as he stood to greet the returning special operative team. At least that was what his mother called it whenever they did anything sneaky like break someone out of a mental hospital and bring them to Eldur.

"You could say that." She lowered herself onto the nearest chair. "Is it always so infernally hot here?" She waved a hand in her face, stirring the sweaty tendrils of blue-tipped hair around her temples.

"Afraid so, but we're glad to have you back with us." Toby smiled at the way Gulliver hovered behind Sophie, like he wanted to give her the world but didn't know if she'd accept it.

"Glad to be here." She sighed, leaning her head back against the chair. "I will never get used to leaving one place at night and stepping through a doorway into daylight. It's exhausting."

"We'll find you a room soon," Gulliver murmured behind her. "And some food."

"Darra, honey." Alona studied Sophie's odd choice of clothing. "You're about the same size as Sophie. Could you go get her some clothes? She'll need a few suitable garments while she's visiting."

"No dresses." Sophie managed to lift her head. "Please," she added with a smile.

"A girl after my own heart." Darra scurried off to her rooms.

"We should get Sophie and her little friend here to the healers, Alona," Brea suggested. "I'm sure they've had an awful time at the institute."

"And who do we have here?" Alona beamed at the little boy clinging to Sophie's side.

"I don't know." He looked the queen in the eye. "Who are you?"

Alona laughed and crouched down beside him. "I'm Queen Alona of Eldur. What's your name, darling?"

"Don't have one. What's an Eldur?"

"It's a where not a what," Toby explained.

"How does he not have a name?" Alona frowned up at Brea.

"Never got one." The boy's eyes were round as saucers as he took in everything at once. "This place is pretty. I like it." He plopped down onto the floor at Sophie's feet, refusing to release her hand.

Brea shook her head at Alona. "Long story, sister."

"Dad!" Tia exclaimed when Lochlan rushed into the room with Finn. "I thought you'd gone back to Iskalt with Keir."

"I don't know. Maybe something about my wife and daughter absconding with a human they broke out of a mental hospital made me want to come right back. I thought I might need to check up on them to see if they've gone mental themselves."

Toby shared a look with his father. The two of them were always the reliable ones to Tia and their mother's impulsive streaks.

"It's my fault, Loch." Gulliver took the blame. "We had to help Sophie."

"It's good to see you safe again, Sophie. Why don't we get you and your friend settled so you can rest? Gulliver, come with me and give me the details I'm sure my wife and her daughter will intentionally leave out in their own recount of the night's events."

"It's always *her* daughter when she's done something impulsive," Brea muttered.

"Can't blame him for that, Mom." Toby laughed. "That apple didn't fall far from the tree."

"Oh, you hush." Brea laughed and pulled Toby into a hug. "Your lives would be boring without us, and you both know it."

Gulliver grasped Sophie's hand as they followed Lochlan from the room.

After they had gone, Griffin lumbered into the room, shouldering a nearly unconscious human onto an empty chair. "This one's going to need some precautionary restraints, Brea."

"On it." Brea murmured a few Fargelsian words, and the arms and legs of the chair moved like vines to wrap around the man's waist and ankles, leaving his hands free for the moment.

"Who's this guy?" Toby frowned at the oddly familiar man. He was certain he'd seen his face before. He looked at Xavier standing beside him. "Do you know this man?"

Xavier nodded. "He's the worldwide leader of HAFS. How on earth did you get your hands on him?"

"Gullie knocked him out with his sword," Tia said proudly.

Toby's eyes widened at that. Gullie was an excellent swordsman, but he abhorred violence of any kind. It wasn't like him to fight unless he'd had no other choice.

"It appears we all have a lot to discuss." Alona sank down onto her chair under a wide window overlooking the palace grounds and the canyon of Radu City far below.

"This man has a lot to answer for." Orla spoke for the first time, her eyes blazing with fury. "Many fae lives have been lost because of him and his father."

Toby stepped between Orla and the man in question. He could see it in her eyes, she was out for blood, but if he really was the leader of HAFS, then they needed this man if they ever wanted a chance of finding peace with the humans.

"I think he's coming around," Alona said. "Tia, get the man some tea and something to eat."

Tia moved to the sideboard on the other side of the room, heated water for tea, and stacked a platter high with little sandwiches and pastries. She brought enough for everyone and set it on the table in front of the strange human.

"Here. Have some tea." Tia poured hot water over a spicy Eldurian blend of black tea, with cinnamon and cardamom and plenty of sugar. "Take it easy. You've had a pretty nasty bump on the head."

She placed the teacup in his hand.

His eyes scanned the room, taking in all the fae beaming welcoming smiles at him.

"Wha ... what's happening?" He closed his eyes and groaned. "Where am I?"

"You're in Eldur," Alona said softly. "Take a moment to get your bearings."

The man's eyes opened wide with fright, followed by anger as he flung the teacup at Tia.

Quicker than a blink, she lifted her hands to block the scalding hot tea with her magic. "Hey! That was hot!" She guided the tea back into the cup and it settled down gently on the table.

"Devils!" the man spat, struggling against the bindings Brea had placed as a precaution.

"Please calm down and tell us your name." Toby raised his voice.

"It's Doctor Clarkson," Brea said softly, the restraints tightening around the human. "He looked just like his father, and I knew him all too well."

"Wicked heathens. Take me back to the institute this instant!"

"I'm afraid we can't do that," Alona apologized. "Brea, you're suffocating him. Relax."

"You will not hold me against my will!" The doctor nearly tipped the chair over in his agitation. "And you will not use your vile magic on me."

"We kind of have to if you want to go home," Toby offered. "And I will be happy to take you there just as soon as the moon rises. If you'll just speak calmly with us, I am certain we can come to an understanding."

"How dare you abduct me from my place of work. This is an act of war." Spittle flew from his mouth. "You will never take our world. I will not have it."

"We don't want it," Tia blurted. "Not that it isn't nice and all, but we have our own world to look after. And just so we're clear ... how is bringing you here any different form you all taking innocent fae into your awful asylum to experiment on?"

"You are an abomination. I will not be held captive by such wicked creatures!"

Tia shared a look with Toby, her face asking the obvious question of whether or not they were dealing with a person of sound mind.

"Doctor, we don't want to hold you captive." Toby stepped forward. "The restraints were a precaution. If you'll just calm down, I am sure we can speak civilly."

"He doesn't know how to speak with a civil tongue." Orla sneered at the man. "He only understands violence."

"Well, we will not be answering violence with violence," Alona said. "If you cannot calm down so we can negotiate a peace with you and your people, then we will never reach an end to this struggle. We want nothing of the human world. We only want the fae living among you to be treated well."

"It's not going to work, Alona." Brea moved to stand in front of the doctor. "His family has never listened to anyone they deem beneath them. And he will never see anyone with magic as a person to be treated with respect. Don't waste your breath."

"You!" The doctor looked up at Toby's mother. "You died when you were just a girl. Your parents insisted they took care of it."

Brea tilted her head, eying the doctor with wary eyes. "What do you mean my parents took care of it? They relinquished their parental rights to the institute after I accidentally used my magic on Myles."

The doctor snorted a laugh. "They did no such thing. The

Robinsons were determined to fix you, even after you killed your friend."

"I didn't kill him. Myles is King Consort of Fargelsi." She crossed her arms over her chest. "See, we treat humans and half-humans here a lot better than you treat the fae in your realm."

"Your idiot parents believed they could rid you of your erratic magic. They wanted that more than anything in the world."

"My parents hated me." Brea frowned.

"Oh, they cared for you, Brea Robinson." The doctor's face broke into a menacing smile. "They cared far too much for their abomination of a daughter. When you escaped with your fae friends, they went after you. We were told they caught up with you and did the right thing."

"Which was what?" Brea demanded.

"They were supposed to have put a bullet through your brain, but I see they utterly failed."

"My parents knew I was fae? They were involved with HAFS?"

"They brought you to my father the first time you displayed signs of magic. They were worried about you, convinced you were a changeling."

"I was." Brea lifted her head defiantly. "I was the child of two very powerful fae rulers, heir to two thrones and more magic than any other fae ever born, before my daughter became even stronger. And you convinced me I was crazy." Her hands clenched into fists. "You could have told me what I was, but you made me question my own sanity."

Her voice shook with emotion, and together, Toby and Tia stepped up beside their mother to comfort her.

"It's okay, Mom." Tia took Brea's hand in hers. "It's all in the past, where it belongs."

"Griff, Xavier, I think it's time we take our guest to his rooms." Toby didn't take his eyes off the doctor. "Perhaps he will feel like discussing options for peace after a good night's rest."

"We'll take him to the dungeons." Xavier stepped forward.

"No. We won't treat him the way he has treated us. Take him to one of the guest suites, but place a guard at his door. For his protection." Toby wrapped an arm around Brea's waist. "He's done enough damage here for one day."

Chapter Seventeen
GULLIVER

Brea's eyes flashed with pain, and Gulliver couldn't seem to shake the faraway look she'd had since she laid eyes on Doctor Clarkson. Ever since he was a child, he'd known her as the warrior queen, the strong and stubborn woman who could vex Lochlan O'Shea and get away with it. The girl who once had two princes in love with her.

"Do you think she's okay?" He looked back over his shoulder as he left the sitting room with Tia by his side.

Tia sighed. "She's insisting she's fine. But it can't be easy for her."

"So you believe she'll be all right?"

"I don't know. My mom ... she had a rough childhood. I

can't imagine living in a place where magic is nothing more than a curse. They hate our kind, Gul. How do we reason with people who lock up children just for being fae? For years, they let her think she was losing her mind. They let her think her parents abandoned her."

Sliding an arm around her shoulders, he hesitated before responding. "Are you so sure we can reason with HAFS?"

"I can't think like that. There has to be a way to stop all of this, to live in peace."

"If you find it, let me know." He hugged her to his side, his tail patting circles on her back.

"We will find a way and we'll do it together. All of us."

Her head dropped onto his shoulder. "Being in charge is exhausting." She pushed him away with sudden strength. "Don't just stand here talking to me, you bumbling fool."

"Whoa, talk about mood change."

She stomped her foot in a very unqueen-like way. "There is a pretty girl who you just freed an entire hospital of prisoners to save sitting in the healing ward. Doctor Clarkson isn't important right now; she is. So why are you standing here with me?"

He wasn't sure what to say to that. Leaning down, he dropped his voice. "I kissed her."

"What?" Tia's eyes lifted to his. "I didn't catch that."

"I kissed Sophie," he said louder this time. "Well, actually she kissed me, but I kissed her back." A few servants stopped in the hall for a moment when he yelled but then continued on their way.

Tia, on the other hand, grinned like she'd known all along. "Of course you did. I'd be very disappointed in you if you hadn't."

He turned away from her. "Walking away now."

"Go get 'em, tiger!"

"I'm not a tiger." He waved over his shoulder. "And all I want is her."

She said the strangest things sometimes.

Most days, walking through the Eldurian palace was a wonder with the courtyards, fountains, and bright artwork, but today the long halls and crisscrossing corridors were nothing more than the distance standing between him and Sophie.

When he finally reached the arched doorway that led to the expansive healing ward, he stopped. Sophie sat on the edge of a feather bed in a pair of Darra's black leather riding pants and a long red tunic. Her blue-tipped hair was pulled back with a white ribbon. And she was beautiful. Despite her human heritage, she fit in this world.

It was more of a feeling than any look that made her blend in. Clothes could change, even demeanor could be refined—just like Brea—but a person's soul ... that was constant. And Sophie's soul was content. He could see it in her eyes, in the way her legs swung happily, her bare toes grazing the stone floor.

Her eyes were on the high ceilings with the exposed beams and arched stone. She didn't look at him before she spoke. "This place is even cooler than Iskalt."

His brow furrowed. "It's very hot. I don't think I'd say it was cool at all."

She lowered her gaze, one eyebrow raised. "You're kind of adorable."

His face flamed at that, so he brushed it aside and walked toward her bed. The boy was nowhere to be found, and neither were the two palace healers. Even the servants seemed to have left them alone. It was a rare moment of peace among the busy kingdoms.

"How are you?" He flinched at how idiotic the question sounded. How was she? Probably not good. She'd just spent too much time in an institute where they did magic knew what to her.

She cut off his thoughts with a simple, "I'm not sure." That was fair. He wasn't exactly sure how he was either.

A piece of hair fell loose from the ribbon, and she tucked it back. "It's nice to be clean. They even took me to a room with the biggest bathtub I've ever seen. It was like a pool in the floor, and it had hot running water. I didn't know you all did indoor plumbing here."

You all. It was just another reminder that she was human and he was fae. "In Iskalt, they bring in copper tubs and magically heat the water, but it's much easier here. When I'm home, we just use the kettle and then mix the steaming water in with the cold. My mother doesn't like having servants, so we do everything ourselves."

She nodded like she was imagining it. "Much different from just turning on the shower."

"I enjoy showers in the human realm." Slowly, he took a seat beside her on the bed. "There are a lot of things there I like."

A sad smile played on her lips. "Most of it is overrated. I'd give up all human conveniences for even a sniff at what you have here with your entire family."

A sniff? "I might not try to smell my father. He's always very busy, so doesn't take as many baths as he probably should. And my sisters ... definitely keep your nose away from them."

"That's not what I ... never mind. I didn't know you had sisters. How old are they?"

"Seven and nine. And they're royal pains too."

She smiled. "You love them."

"More than anything. Just don't tell them I said that or I'll never hear the end of it."

Their voices dropped off, and they shared the silence, the sound of their breath the only noise to reach their ears.

One of the healers walked in, his steps echoing off the high ceilings. He crossed the room and exited through another door.

Gulliver released a breath. "I—"

"You kissed me back." Sophie's words were soft but clear.

"You kissed me first." He turned to look at her and found her watching him.

"I didn't expect you to come for me."

"Is that why you kissed me?"

He couldn't breathe while he waited for the answer, not sure what he wanted to hear.

After a few beats, Sophie shook her head. "No. It was because when I was locked up, I missed you. I don't think I realized how much until I saw you."

"You ... missed me? But ..." How? He wasn't like her. With his tail, his eyes ...

"Stop." She touched the side of his face, her fingers gliding across his skin. "I know what you're thinking, Gulliver O'Shea. Isn't it enough to say I thought of you? That you kept me going?"

One corner of his mouth curved up. This was it. He would get to kiss her again, to enjoy it this time and memorize every moment. His eyes flicked to her lips, watched as she released a puff of air.

And then, the whispering came. "Do you think we're interrupting them?"

"Probably. I can't tell. Why are they so close to each other?"

Gulliver closed his eyes for a moment in exasperation, and Sophie laughed. Hearing that sound was worth the interruption. It had been too rare.

He turned to Brea, who stood with a hand on the boy's shoulder.

"Sophie." The boy ran toward her and jumped onto the bed to give her a hug. "I left to explore when the healer wasn't looking, but then I couldn't find my way back." He pulled away, his voice hoarse. "I can't hear you."

"She's right here." Gulliver looked from the boy to Brea, who shrugged.

"He means in his head," Sophie explained, not taking her eyes from him. "I can't hear you either."

"It's like when you disappeared before."

A realization hit her. "When I first came to the fae realm." That was it. Their connection only worked in the human world. "Do you have your magic?"

He shook his head.

"What do you mean?" Alarm hit Gulliver. He'd seen what the boy could do when he threw Griff in the air.

"As soon as we entered the portal, I felt it leave." The boy grinned. "It felt ... like freedom. My magic has only ever caused me problems." He jumped off the bed, tears in his eyes.

Brea pulled him into a motherly hug. If there was one person this kid needed in his life, it was the Queen Mother of Iskalt. "You're safe now," she murmured. "We will protect you."

Sophie reached for Gulliver's hand, as if he could lend her strength. Their fingers intertwined. "He grew up in the institute since he was a baby."

Brea's eyes widened, and tears glistened in their depths. She'd been in and out of the institute for years as a teen but never for long. "How did his parents let that happen?"

The boy looked up at her. "I don't have any parents, ma'am."

"Oh, honey." She hugged him tighter.

"Do I have to go back there?" he asked. "Are you going to

send me back to the humans since my magic doesn't work anymore?"

She put a hand under his chin and tilted his face up. "You listen to me. No one will hurt you again. Your future is now yours to choose. If you wish to stay, there is a place for you here."

Sophie leaned her head on Gulliver's shoulder. Her cheeks were damp, and he wondered if she needed someone to say that to her. Or maybe she wanted to go back and live among her kind. All he knew was, in that moment, he didn't have the courage to ask.

"First order of business." Brea patted the boy's head. "Our new friend doesn't have a name and that won't do."

He sniffed. "I think I'd like having a name. Can I have a dog too?"

A laugh burst out of Brea. "One thing at a time." She leaned down to whisper, "But yes, we may be able to find you a dog."

His grin was so large that Gulliver had to keep himself from blubbering along with Sophie.

Sophie leaned forward to pull the boy to stand in front of her. "What do you feel like? What name fits you?"

His little lips pursed as he considered her question. It was only a minute before his eyes lit up. "One of the nurses used to read to me, and we read every book in the institute's library."

"Wouldn't be hard," Sophie grumbled.

The boy shrugged. "There was one that took us ages to read. It has all sorts of stories. Then, when we finished, we read it a couple more times. I think I'd like one of the names of the superheroes in that."

Brea smiled. "Myles had a horse named Captain America once."

"That's a strange name." Gulliver would never understand humans.

Sophie pushed them forward. "So, what's this superhero's name?"

The boy stood up straighter. "Jesus."

The two women were silent, and Gulliver looked between them, unable to read their expressions.

Finally, Brea rubbed the back of her neck. "Kid, do you mean you read the *Bible* over and over?"

"Yes!" He bounced on his toes. "That was the title. Jesus had magic just like me. I always thought I was like him."

Brea tried to stifle her smile, but it didn't work as her lips curved. "I think we should go with your second choice. Jesus is a very famous man."

He shrugged. "Okay. Then ... Noah. He really liked animals. I've never been around them, but I think I'd like animals too."

There was no stopping all their smiles at that.

Gulliver stuck out a hand for him to shake. "Welcome to the fae realm, Noah. Your new home."

Chapter Eighteen

SOPHIE

The lingering effects of the drugs were finally out of her system now. Sophie stared out the window of her beautiful room in the Eldurian palace. The exotic courtyard drew her attention to the tinkling fountains and the palm fronds rustling in the dry desert breeze. Before she retired for the evening, the healers had given her a potion that had strengthened her body and restored the clarity of her mind. After a nap and a good meal, she and Noah had been given their own rooms.

It was hot, and she couldn't get comfortable as she tossed and turned, her mind whirring with too many thoughts at once. She had so many questions. Questions about her father and how her mother died. Questions about her past. Uncertainty about her future.

Shoving the thin cooling blanket aside, she rolled out of bed and reached for the robe Princess Darra had brought her. She didn't know where she was going, but she had to get out of this room and stretch her legs. Too much time in the institute had worn her down physically.

She wandered along corridors and through courtyards, getting lost and found again when she stumbled upon the doctor's room. Guards stood sentry in the hall outside.

Squaring her shoulders, she approached the fae guards. "I'd like to see Doctor Clarkson."

The male guard glanced at his female companion before they stepped aside.

"Call for assistance should you need it." The man nodded as she opened the door.

It was a simple room. Nothing as lavish as the one she'd been given, but it seemed comfortable, which was far more than he deserved.

That he and other members of HAFS couldn't see the fae's kindness baffled her.

"No need to creep around in the dark. I am awake." The doctor sat up from the bed, where he'd been lounging. "I will not rest while among the enemy."

"They aren't the enemy," Sophie said, stepping into the moonlight streaming in from the window above his bed.

"You have fallen under their influence, Sophie. I cannot help you now."

"You think you're helping anyone?" Fury heated her tone. "In your institute of horrors?"

"I do what I can to save the humans who have been tainted by their evil magic."

"They aren't evil! The fae of the five kingdoms are the

kindest souls I've ever known. They are almost childlike in their innocence and ignorance of the evils that humans perpetrate against them. The only thing they are guilty of is their overzealous desire to help, in that it often has the opposite effect."

"You have been duped, you stupid girl. Just like your mother."

"What do you know of my mother?" Sophie took a step closer to Clarkson, searching his face for the answers she needed. There was still so much she didn't know about her mother's death. She knew it was her father who pulled the trigger, but HAFS was behind it.

"She betrayed your father, and she betrayed her kind when she chose a fae abomination over her own family."

"What do mean she chose the fae?" She tilted her head, pretending to be confused. "My mother died when the darkness came."

"You think that's when HAFS began?" The doctor laughed mirthlessly. "My father gathered the first humans to our cause before I was born. The fae have been among us for generations, and they grow stronger and stronger as the years pass. They will take us over when their numbers surpass ours. They want the human world for themselves."

"No," Sophie insisted. "They just want to live in peace."

"Peace?" Clarkson snorted. "You are even more naïve than your mother was. They will breed with humans until they wipe us out completely. Even now, it is difficult to find humans completely untainted by fae blood and their unholy magic."

"What does it even matter?" Sophie threw her hands up, completely bewildered. "We're all people who want the same things in life. Who cares if they have magic we can't understand? You don't see them waging war against us because we have technology they find equally terrifying. The only thing that makes them different is their pointy ears and their truly odd sense of humor."

"You forget your friend with the tail and feline eyes. The fae with wings, horns, or scales like fish. What sort of feral creatures have their ancestors bred with? And now they want to mix with humans? No. We will not have it. I will fight until my last breath to save our world for the humans."

"And kill how many innocents along the way?"

"Innocent lives will always suffer when it comes to war."

Sophie knew she was fighting a losing battle with this man. Hate was ingrained in him. A hate his father had taught him and probably his grandfather before that. Nothing would change that kind of blind willfulness.

"How did my father become involved with HAFS? When?"

"Long before you were even born. He brought your mother into it when they married, though she remained on the outskirts of the group, refusing to take a leadership role like your father."

"And then, the darkness came, and she died."

"The darkness wasn't the harbinger of her death. Her death was her own doing."

"How? Tell me what happened."

"She was unfaithful. But your mother loved you." Clarkson met her gaze for the first time. 'I believe you were the only reason she stayed in an unhappy marriage for as long as she did."

"She loved my father." Sophie knew deep in her soul that her mother had once loved Claude Devereaux. She'd watched her father mourn her mother for more than a decade. He was lost without her. Surely she must have returned that same devotion before HAFS came between them.

"She did, in the beginning. As Claude rose in rank through

the years, she resisted. She wasn't happy when he became the leader of HAFS in New Orleans. But she stayed. For you."

"My father always said magic killed my mother." Tears burned her eyes, but she refused to shed them. Not when she was so close to having the answers to so many questions.

The doctor laughed at that. "I suppose, in a way, it did."

"I remember when she died. There was a loud noise and a flash of light, like headlights. And then, she was gone. The fae killed her that night."

But it wasn't them. Maybe her father had talked about it so much she remembered his version of what happened that night.

"She got herself killed when she fell in love with an abomination."

"Love?" Sophie blinked back her tears. "She had an affair with a half-fae?" It all made sense now. Of course her father would have lost his mind over that.

The doctor nodded. "He had strange magic, even for the fae. He looked human. That's how they work their way into human lives, hiding what they are."

"And she wanted to leave?" She ignored his narrowminded waffle.

Clarkson nodded again. "She wanted to leave Claude and take you to live among the fae." He snorted a laugh, as if that was the most ridiculous thing he'd ever heard. "She lost her mind." He shook his head. "HAFS had to step in to save her, but she wouldn't hear of it. She stayed in the institute for a while, and it soon became clear she was expecting another child. A fae child."

Sophie gasped. "She had a baby?"

"She was mad for her lover and their child. He helped her escape, and they were going to run away together, the three of them. But she wouldn't leave you."

Sophie's mind reeled with this information. "And it got her killed, didn't it? HAFS killed her."

Except, it was Claude who'd done it. That was the part that never made sense to her. Since the night she'd overheard her father and the doctor talking about her mother's death, Sophie couldn't figure out how her dad had found it within himself to actually kill her mother. But jealousy? She could see it now.

"Claude took her home and kept her away from her lover. After the child was born, she tried to leave again. She took the baby and tried to pick you up from school. She was going to leave that night, though she had no car, no money, or means to travel. Her bags were packed, and it seemed as though she intended to walk out of the city with an infant and a young child."

"I remember that day." Sophie choked on her words. "The darkness had just started to creep across the city. Mom came to get me from school early." She frowned. "I don't remember the baby, but I had to be at least eight or nine years old by then. I should have remembered him."

"Your father encouraged you to forget him ... after."

She shook her head. "This doesn't make any sense."

Sophie studied the doctor's face, searching for signs of his lies.

"Claude went after her. He knew what had to be done. We never tolerate dissension among our ranks."

"And he killed her for it." Sophie shook her head again.

"It was your father's responsibility to deal with her treachery. Your mother wasn't well, Sophie. It had to be done."

"Wasn't well?" she whispered. "Because she had the audacity to fall in love with someone not quite human?"

"They are vile creatures. They must be stopped. And when a human is too far gone, there is only one answer."

"Murder?" She glared at him; her fists clenched at her sides.

"Claude loved your mother. He did what he had to do to save her soul."

"No." She stepped away from the doctor. "He was a jealous fool."

"He was a fool. He couldn't bring himself to kill her child," Clarkson continued, a gleam of triumph in his eye. "So, he brought the boy to the institute."

"Noah," Sophie gasped as she sank to the floor. "He's my brother."

"The boy was fae. A disgrace. He wasn't your brother. He wasn't human."

"What did you do to his magic?" She thought about the doctor's machines. The same ones that ripped through her, searching for traces of magic. What had Noah experienced in a lifetime at their hands?

"We couldn't rid him of magic, but we diminished it."

"Diminished?" What must Noah have been capable of before they tampered with his magic? "You're monsters." She scooted across the floor toward the door, unable to get her feet under her as her body trembled with so much emotion she couldn't identify all she was feeling. Anger, sadness, and so much rage. "You tried to break him."

"And we did. His magic is erratic and dangerous now. He can't be allowed to roam free. But the boy has given us valuable information on the genetic makeup of fae. Through him, we have learned to identify the markers of those with magic and those without. We will eradicate all magic from our world in one way or another. And then, we will go after every human with even a drop of fae blood until our world is pure again."

"You're disgusting. All of you are past redemption. You'll never be satisfied with peace, so why should we even try?" In that moment, Sophie set her father free. Nothing he could say or do could ever make up for the damage he'd done to their family. She'd never doubted his love, but she could never condone his actions. He would have to bear the responsibility for those actions all on his own.

Her mother had another child. A beautiful boy whose terrifying magic seemed to be tempered in the fae world. Noah was her family now, and she would do right by him.

"You're a silly child, Sophie Devereaux. HAFS will never settle for peace with the fae. We will take the world back for the humans. And anyone who stands in our way will not stand for long."

Sophie reached for the arm of a nearby chair and pulled herself up. She wiped her eyes and gave the doctor one long last look. "You will not win this war."

She turned and left him to his delusions.

Sleep would never come to her now. Searching the rooms nearest to hers, she found Noah sleeping soundly in one just across the courtyard.

She imagined any other ten-year-old would be too terrified to sleep in a strange bed in a strange land, but not her brother. She sat beside him, watching him sleep with a sweet smile on his face.

"I won't let anyone hurt you ever again." She brushed her fingertips over his forehead, smoothing back his soft curls so she could study his face for signs of their mother.

She saw her in the shape of his eyes and the curve of his mouth. In his sweet disposition and his uncanny ability to make the best out of the worst situations.

She traced a finger along his hairline, the soft dark blond curls much like their mother's.

And Sophie smiled when she noticed the subtle point of his little ears that he got from his father.

Chapter Nineteen
GULLIVER

"You'll like it, I promise." Gulliver slid a steaming mug of Eldur brew across the pub table. "Brea says it's a lot like the humans' coffee drink, but I've never been fond of the taste. It's a little too bitter for me, but it's popular among the working class in Eldur. Probably because it'll wake you up so fast you might not blink for hours."

"Says the fae who gets drunk off a few sips of wine." Tia snickered, but Gulliver kicked her under the table. He was dorky enough on his own and didn't need his best friend helping him look even more foolish in front of Sophie.

"You should try the chocoah." Tia wrinkled her nose at the Eldur brew. "We've just started importing it from Lenya, and it's so good. We can't get enough of it at the palace. It's like human hot chocolate, but even better. It tastes like chocolate, but creamier and sweeter." She dipped her head to sip from the brimming mug in front of her. She sat back with a full chocoah mustache she wiped away with her hand.

"Can I try both?" Sophie eyed the frothing sweet drink Tia was slurping down. "I bet they'd be amazing if you mixed them. It would sweeten up the coffee with the chocolate and dial down the bitterness while making the chocoah a little less sweet."

"Oh." Tia's eyes widened. "That actually sounds delicious." She leaned over the table to get the barmaid's attention and ordered two more of each drink.

"Might be even better iced too," Sophie suggested.

"Ow. What was that for?" Gulliver gripped his shin where Tia had kicked him under the table.

"I like her. Don't screw it up."

"Stop talking, Tia," Gulliver growled

"We were hoping marriage and a crown would force her to grow up." Toby rolled his eyes. "No such luck."

"You're right, the Eldur brew stuff is a lot like coffee," Xavier admitted, clearly trying to change the subject back. "Just not as good."

"It's a little too bitter," Sophie agreed. "But it'll do in a pinch."

"My mom says that a lot," Tia said. "But as much as I love humanisms, that one has never made any sense. Who's doing the pinching? And why?"

"As lively as this conversation is, that's not what we came all the way down here to discuss." Gulliver looked over his shoulder at the other pub patrons, minding their own business. "Are you sure this is the best place to talk?"

"I used to come here a lot with Logan and Darra. The pub

owner will chase away anyone who gets too nosey." Toby nodded at the man behind the bar. "We can talk. Just keep your voices down." He looked at Tia as he spoke.

"Why do you say that like I'm the loud one?" She scowled at her brother.

"Because you *are* the loud one." Gulliver sipped his chocoah, thinking he agreed with Sophie. The sweet drink might benefit from some of the bitterness of Eldur beans.

She was better since her arrival in Eldur. More focused and decisive. She hadn't said as much, but Gulliver got the feeling she'd left a lot of her past behind her at the Clarkson Institute. She just woke up her second morning here and seemed to have a lot more determination. Most of which was directed at protecting Noah.

"Peace talks are only going to work if both parties are interested," Xavier began. "And I don't know if we have the kind of time that will take to convince Clarkson to even consider a truce."

"We don't," Sophie said. "And he won't ever consider it. That man can't be reasoned with."

"So, what do we do if one side of this situation refuses to negotiate?" Toby asked.

"It's not just fae verses human, though," Sophie said. "There are three sides here, and we're trying to reason with only one of them."

Gulliver forced himself to focus on all her words and not just the part where she lumped herself in with the fae. She thought of them as a *we*, and that made him feel all sorts of emotions he wasn't ready to think about yet. Not that he had time for such things.

"What do you mean?" Tia asked.

"She's talking about HAFS," Gulliver offered.

"I thought that's what we were talking about." Tia frowned. "Doctor Clarkson is the head of HAFS."

"He is, but he isn't the leader of all humans. Only those who believe the fae are evil magic wielders waiting to gobble up their world. Not all humans are like him."

"Unfortunately, HAFS are behind the strikes against the fae communities in our world." Xavier leaned against the table, leaving his drink forgotten.

"But now that the human government has become involved in the fight for Los Angeles, the information people are getting is filtered through the hate of HAFS," Sophie said. "It's like your everyday human has just realized HAFS was right all along, so now they're listening to everything they say, believing it must be the truth.

"We need a way to get the real truth out to the non-HAFS humans." As Sophie talked, Gullie leaned in to hang on her every word. "A way to help them see fae aren't the monsters they've been led to believe they are."

"But how can we do that?" Tia's voice sounded distant, like she was thinking deeply while she poured Eldur brew into her chocoah mug and sloshed it around before she took a hesitant sip.

"Hmmm, that is good, Soph." She lifted her mug, and Gulliver shook his head at his best friend. Maybe her thoughts weren't so deep after all.

"Focus, Tia." Gulliver slapped his hand on the table to get her attention.

"What? I am." She took another sip. "We need a way to talk directly to the human population. To get past HAFS."

"Well..." Sophie shared a look with Xavier. "We could do that."

"The media?" Xavier let out an anxious sigh. "That could go badly for us if we aren't careful."

"So, we'll be careful," Sophie said. "Find the right person to talk to, someone who won't twist your words to make it fit their agenda."

"We should talk to Orla," Toby suggested. "She might know of someone we could trust."

"She does know someone." Xavier nodded, a smile spreading across his face. "She has a cousin who is mostly human, no magic of any kind, but she's sympathetic to the fae."

"How will that help?" Gulliver asked, not seeing how a sympathetic human could help them get on the human feletision.

"She's a reporter in L.A., and people love her. Most would never know she had fae blood."

Tia chewed on her bottom lip for a moment before she spoke. "Could she get me on the televisions so I could talk to the humans?"

Chapter Twenty
TOBY

This was either a really terrible idea or the best one they'd had in a long time.

"What does this do?" Gulliver reached for a piece of equipment, and two humans simultaneously yelled for him to stop. It was too late. He stumbled, startled by their noise, and knocked into the black box on a stick in front of him.

It crashed to the floor, leaving the entire room in an air of shocked silence.

Gulliver's face went bright red. "Oops."

"Hey, Gul." Brea put a maternal hand on his back. "Let's move away from the cameras, yeah?"

He nodded sullenly and followed her.

Tia could barely contain her laughter as Orla and Xavier scrambled to right the camera and make sure it wasn't broken, issuing apologies as they did.

There were six of them who'd traveled from the fae realm. The two half-fae rebels, Brea, Tia, Gulliver, and Toby. It was too dangerous for Sophie to come all the way here, so she'd meet them at the farmhouse with Griff when all of this was done.

Toby turned to take in what Xavier had called a news studio. There was a desk behind the cameras with spots for two humans. He'd seen the news before, but this was different, more somehow. The people who worked here told the rest of the human world what was happening and what they should believe. It was a kind of power he'd never imagined.

"Kind of cool, right?" Xavier joined him, a hesitant smile on his face.

Toby hated himself for putting that hesitation there. His conflicting emotions about Logan shouldn't have made Xavier doubt himself. They were friends, of course they were. But though neither had acknowledged it, there was also something more. When Toby was with Xavier, he could hope again. Plan for a future that had felt so dark and lonely for too long.

There were still bruises on Xavier's olive skin from the battle in Aghadoon, a new scar above his left eye. Yet, he was the same man who'd seen two out-of-their-element fae in New Orleans and tried to help them.

Toby realized he hadn't responded, so he nodded. "It's very ... human."

He would never admit this to his sister or his parents, but he loved the human world. Not the evil here, but the way a person didn't need magic to have worth. Their magic was in the technology that was available to all.

He fit in here among the half-fae in a way he didn't back home.

"Is that a bad thing?" Xavier didn't sound defensive, only curious.

Toby thought for a moment. "No. Just different."

Like him.

Having no magic other than the O'Shea portal ability made him an outsider among his own people. He knew they tried not to see him as such, but it was impossible. Even Tia, who often needed him to be her amplifier, sometimes looked at him with pity.

Xavier lifted a hand, but let it drop, and Toby wanted to know what he was going to do. Give him a friendly pat on the shoulder? Touch his cheek? Take his hand?

Whatever it was, Toby wanted to lean into him. Alona had been right. Logan wouldn't want him to grieve forever. Yet, it wasn't that simple. It never was.

"I'm sorry." The words came before he realized he'd spoken them.

Xavier's brow furrowed. "You're sorry ..."

"For avoiding you, not telling you why. I've made so many mistakes."

Xavier's hand brushed the back of Toby's. "I know about Logan." He waited a beat before continuing. "I'm so sorry, Tobes. If I could give him back to you and disappear, I would."

"What if I don't want you to disappear?"

They stared at each other for a long moment, and Toby didn't breathe, couldn't breathe.

Their standoff ended when a black woman with long, beautiful curls walked out and clapped her hands. "Are we ready to change the world?"

Toby was momentarily stunned by the woman who must have been Orla's cousin. She had a face made for the human televisions, with sparkling white teeth, a bright and genuine smile, and deep green eyes.

Orla greeted her with a kiss on each cheek before turning to the group. "Everyone, this is Stella. Her cameraman is named Bones."

"Bones?" Tia chuckled under her breath.

Orla shot her a look. "They're risking a lot for this. They've made sure the rest of their crew is away for the night and locked the doors so no one else can get in. We need to record this quickly. She'll put it on the air in the morning."

It made sense now, why they had to wait until the dead of night to come in. The other humans who worked here didn't know what was happening.

Orla walked Stella toward Tia and Brea. "These two will be going on the air."

Stella adjusted a piece of plastic that rested on her head, stretching toward her mouth. "Welcome, your Majesty." She directed the greeting to Brea.

Brea laughed. "Oh dear, I convinced my husband to get me out of that role the moment my daughter was ready. Tia here is the Iskaltian queen now."

Stella nodded, not correcting herself. "I have a friend who will air this overseas with subtitles in French, Spanish, and Chinese. Do you have preferred pronouns so we can get the introduction, right?"

Tia looked at her mother in confusion.

Toby didn't know the answer to that either. What was a pronoun? Why was it important?

Orla put a hand on Stella's shoulder. "Let's not break their fae brains. Put them down for she/her."

"Got it. I just always want to be sensitive." She walked back toward the camera to speak with Bones.

Orla rubbed her eyes. "It's hard to grasp that the fae world doesn't understand the human way of life. Do you two know what you're going to say?"

Tia shrugged. "Figured I'd wing it. That's what humans would call it, right?"

Brea rolled her eyes. "Yes, we're prepared. Ignore my daughter."

Orla nodded. "Well, we have a lot of lives riding on this."

Toby's chest tightened as their conversation finished.

"How do your mom and sister have so much faith in a president they know nothing about?" Xavier asked.

Toby couldn't take his eyes from the confidence in Tia's posture. He'd questioned so many of her decisions in life, but this was the right one. "They're both queens. They know what it is to have the well-being of an entire kingdom on their shoulders. It's less faith and more hope that the human leader has even an ounce of what they do."

"And what's that?"

"Love for their people."

Stella gestured for the two women to join her. She positioned them both in front of a giant green wall. It would look odd on camera, but Toby figured she knew what she was doing.

Toby went to Gulliver at the side of the stage to watch them. Tia stuck her tongue out at him, and he sighed.

"We're seriously putting the fate of our people in that girl's hands?" Orla shook her head. "I think we've all gone mad."

Toby's jaw clenched, but Gulliver beat him to a response.

"That *girl* is a queen. She deserves to be treated as such. And she has saved more fae than you can even fathom exist. So, yes, your fate is in her hands, and you should be darn glad it is."

Toby patted his back in solidarity. He was glad Tia had Gulliver. After Logan died, when he couldn't be there for her, she'd still had a brother. Toby had allowed his grief to swallow him whole, but it hadn't left her alone.

His pinky hooked around Xavier's, not quite handholding but almost. When Xavier didn't pull away, Toby smiled.

This would work. It had to.

Bones lifted a hand and Stella yelled, "Everyone quiet!"

One of Bones' fingers dropped, then another, until finally, he pointed the last one at the two queens.

Neither of them spoke.

Stella cursed. "That means start."

"Oh." Tia bounced on her toes like she couldn't contain her nervous energy. "Well, hello there."

Toby slapped a hand to his forehead.

"Chill, Tia." Brea took her hand.

"You chill, Mom." Tia ripped it away. "You don't get to tell me what to do anymore, remember? I'm your queen."

"You're my daughter first."

They'd had this argument more times than Toby could count. "For magic's sake, can my family just act normal for once?"

They both looked at him and straightened, taking it as a challenge. They were the same person, and it was never more evident than in that moment.

Tia turned to look at the camera, and Brea followed suit.

"Hello, humans." Tia smiled, trying to look normal, but it actually seemed like she'd lost her mind.

Brea's smile was more natural as she said, "I was one of you once. Well, I thought I was. I lived in ignorance of the fae, not even knowing of their existence. You know about us, so yay!"

Tia rolled her eyes. "My name is Tierney O'Shea. I am one of the queens of the fae, and I've come here to beg your mercy. Our people are suffering. From bombings in your cities to all-out war, we are dying. And so are humans. None of us want this. The fae have only ever wanted peace."

Brea picked up where she left off. "I spent the first seventeen years of my life in the human realm before becoming a queen of the fae. I know how terrifying it is to learn of magic and the kinds of abilities those different from you have. It probably scares you as much as technology scares my husband. You should see a fae catch sight of a car for the first time." She doubled over in laughter.

Toby coughed, trying to remind his mother to maintain some semblance of seriousness.

Brea's face sobered. "We don't want to fight. All we want is safety for those fae and half-fae who live in your world."

"For that," Tia started, "we must speak to your leader. To the queen of the United America—"

"President of the United States of America," Brea coughed.

"—and you are watching this, know that we wish to meet, ruler to ruler. We are prepared to negotiate for peace, for an end to the fighting. All we want is an end to the terrorist group known as HAFS that is destroying cities in their search for fae."

"Yes." Brea stepped closer to the camera. "Take me to your leader." Her voice sounded odd.

Tia yanked her back. "But like, in a non-terrifying way." She side-eyed their mom. "There is an address we will give to the representative of the president. Call this number." She rattled off the number Orla set up for this purpose. "We hope to hear from you." She nodded once and walked off the stage.

Brea was still laughing as she approached Toby. "I've always wanted to say that. 'Take me to your leader'." Tears danced in her eyes.

"Why are you like this, Mom?" He bit back a smile, the kind she always seemed to be able to pull out of him.

She wrapped an arm around his shoulder and guided him toward the door. "Because, kiddo, life shouldn't be so serious all the time. Sometimes, we just have to enjoy the moment when we don't know how many more we'll get together."

As she dragged him away, he glanced back at Xavier. The other man walked with his hands deep in his pockets, his shoulders hunched.

Toby wanted to enjoy his moments too.

Chapter Twenty-One

SOPHIE

Tension filled the farmhouse. Two days ago, the message to the President aired. Sophie was the only one who hadn't believed the woman would actually come to a farmhouse in Ohio. She was the President of the United States, after all. A title that meant little to the fae. Their leaders were much more accessible, less guarded.

"Stop pacing," Tia snapped at her brother.

Toby ignored her.

There were too many people crowded into the small living room, too little space. Sophie could hardly breathe.

Xavier crossed the room, sliding his hand into Toby's and dragging him toward the hallway for a break.

She wondered if anyone else saw it. The way the two men cast glances at each other, looking away when their eyes met.

They were falling in love.

Just like she was. Minute by minute, day by day. Every touch, every smile, every time she heard Gulliver say her name in that whispery way of his.

Right now, she wasn't sure why. Gulliver and Tia had raided the fridge as soon as they ran in the door and now sat side by side in a pile of wrappers, crumbs coating their shirts. Gulliver had Nutella smeared on his lips, and Tia had dripped sauce from a hot pocket onto her pants.

In other words, they were a wreck as they waited for a call from the most influential person in the free world.

At least Kier wasn't here to watch Tia sink into her food coma. He was back in Iskalt making sure the kingdom didn't fall into the icy seas or something. Gulliver told her about a wicked storm off the coast to the north, but she hadn't completely understood what he was talking about.

Tia burped as Griff took a spot leaning against the wall beside Sophie. "I'm sorry."

That surprised her. "For what?"

"Not teaching my son how to not be gross."

A laugh escaped her. "It's okay. Certain foods here are ... addictive."

"He's going to miss them." She got the feeling he wasn't only talking about the food.

She had so many decisions to make. Was there a place for her anymore among the humans? Would her brother come back here with her?

Brother. She still hadn't gotten used to that thought, but she wished he was here with her. The only thing she knew was that it would always be her and Noah.

"What's it like?" she asked. "Having a brother?"

Griff didn't answer for a long moment before he sighed. "I spent most of my life hating Lochlan. We were raised separately, as enemies. It wasn't until I'd spent a decade in the prison realm, been forgotten by the world, and then helped them restore memories and destroy the dark king that we even got a chance to be family."

"Whoa." That was ... dark. "And now?"

"We're figuring it out still. I think we always will be. But I can now say I wouldn't want to live my life without my brother and his family. When it's good, it's a love unlike anything else."

A smile curved her lips. She couldn't wait for a lifetime getting to know Noah. "And Gullie? You two truly love each other, don't you?"

Griff wasn't his biological father, but what they had was so very different from the controlling relationship her own father created. She hadn't seen it at the time when her father was sitting beside her hospital bed for years, taking care of her.

Griff gave her a sad smile. "You could have this, Sophie."

He gestured around the room where Tia and her father were arguing. Brea was watching them like it was a soccer match. Gulliver was half asleep. She knew Griff meant not only those present, but their family who wasn't here. Kier, Gulliver's mother and sisters, the royal family she'd met in Eldur.

"I know." Tears flooded her eyes because it was true. They'd welcome her and Noah with open arms. It was who they were. But she wasn't fae. Did she belong in their world?

"Take it from me, Sophie. Sometimes, a family is made, not born." He left her with those words and approached the couch, shoving Gulliver's head to wake him up. He sat with a start and scowled at his father.

The front door banged open, and Orla sprinted in, holding

a ringing phone in her hand. It was a prepaid phone she'd bought for a single purpose.

The President's call.

Tia jumped to her feet. "Answer it!"

Toby and Xavier rushed back in to join them as Orla put the phone on speaker. "Hello?" she said.

A low voice responded. "The President of the United States will arrive in five minutes."

Then, they hung up.

The room burst into chatter.

"They were supposed to call and ask where to meet!" Tia's eyes held panic.

"How did they know where we were?" Toby asked.

They didn't understand the true power of the President. They could find out anything. And now, she was on her way to a small, broken-down farmhouse in Ohio full of chaos and confusion. And a fae queen with pizza stains on her pants.

No, this wouldn't do.

Sophie pushed off the wall. "Everyone shut up!"

They kept talking.

This wasn't working. Searching the room, she found a small end table and climbed onto it. "Quiet!"

This time, they looked at her, their talk dying away. She wanted to wither under their stares, but she couldn't back down now.

"I have gone through too much at the hands of HAFS for this meeting to fail." She jumped off the table. "Xavier and Toby, make sure there's a comfortable place for her to sit. Orla, go into the kitchen and put a kettle on. Gulliver, get the crumbs off your shirt. Tia, try to act like a queen, and for Fae's sake, go change your pants!" She turned to Brea and Lochlan, the latter scowling.

"Go on, honey." Brea smiled. "I'm quite enjoying this.

Don't stop when it's my husband's turn. He loves being told what to do."

Somehow, she didn't believe her. "Sir," Sophie started, trying to keep her voice from shaking, "the Secret Service will most likely come first. You should go greet them."

"What's a Secret Service?" he asked, crossing his arms.

Brea laughed. "You're going to love them, Loch. They won't make you angry at all."

"Brea, can you—"

"Take care of the President?" Brea finished.

Sophie didn't admit that was exactly what she was going to say.

Brea nodded in excitement. "This is the highlight of my little human heart."

"You don't have a human heart, Mom." Tia rolled her eyes as she practiced her posture.

"I once thought I did."

"I don't get it." Gulliver stood and shook his entire body so the crumbs fell off. His tail finished dusting off his shirt. "Why are you acting weird, Soph?"

How could he not get it? "The President is coming. Here. Like right now and there are candy wrappers everywhere!"

"So? My best friend is a queen."

They would never understand.

A heavy knock sounded on the door, and Lochlan, like an obedient man, went to open it.

Two large men in black suits pushed him aside and rushed into the room. Another was outside, circling the farmhouse.

"Clear!" one of the men yelled from another room. A few more rounds of 'clear' rang out with the men not saying a word to them. Lochlan was already fuming.

"Told you that you'd like them." Brea patted her husband's back.

The two men reappeared in the living room, one of them looking like he was talking to himself.

"Which one of you are the President?" Gulliver asked.

Neither responded.

Tia stood, her spine ramrod straight. She put on her stern queen face. "You can't just barge into the human farmhouse of a fae queen."

Sophie looked away to hide her smile. Sometimes, the fae were too adorable.

The front door opened again, and the third agent gestured to a black town car rolling down the gravel drive, dust kicking up in its wake.

Chapter Twenty-Two
GULLIVER

Gulliver stood on one side of the door, waiting with Griffin for the human queen to get out of her car. She seemed in no hurry to come inside. The men who came in first were still running around, checking every nook and cranny of the house—for what, Gulliver couldn't fathom.

"All clear for the Falcon to fly,' one of the men in dark suits told his wrist.

"Humans are a strange lot, aren't they?" Griff scratched his head as he watched the woman exit the rear seat of the sleek black car. It was nicer than anything Gulliver had ever ridden in, that was for sure.

"Madame President, they are ready for you." Two more suited men escorted the woman up to the front porch. She gave the house a once over, and her delicate nose wrinkled as she removed a pair of dark glasses from their perch.

"And this is where they chose to meet?" She eyed the holes in the screen door. "Odd choice for diplomatic negotiations."

"I'm told their queen grew up in this house, ma'am."

"The queen's mother did," Gulliver shouted through the screen. "At least, one of the fae queens, I mean."

"And you are?" The human queen, president, whatever stepped into the kitchen, her suited guards leading the way.

"Gulliver, your Majesty." He bowed his head. "Er, Lord Gulliver O'Shea, I mean. Ma'am." He gave a little salute the way he'd seen the human soldiers do.

"Lord?" She arched a brow at him.

"My son, your Majesty." Griffin bowed. "Prince Griffin O'Shea of Iskalt." He offered his arm, but her guards closed in on her, not allowing the propriety.

"You have more than one ... kingdom?" she asked.

"Last count was five, your Majesty," Gulliver offered. "But they tend to crop up out of nowhere from time to time."

"I see. And each of these kingdoms has a monarch?"

"Yes, your Majesty." Gulliver bowed again.

"I am not a queen." The woman's voice was very cold and unyielding.

"Please refer to the President as either Madame President, ma'am, or President Worthington," one of her guards explained.

"Yes, ma'am." Gulliver nodded once again. "Each kingdom has a king or queen. You will meet with her Majesty Queen Tierney O'Shea of Iskalt. My sort of cousin-sister and best friend."

"Oh, dear." The President clutched a hand to her heart.

Griff cleared his throat. "What my son means is, he is adopted and I am Tierney's natural father. I was once married to the former queen of Iskalt. But she's now married to my brother, who raised Tierney and her twin brother."

"And that's more information than President Worthington needed to know." Brea stepped into the kitchen, extending her hand to the President, but the guards wouldn't let her approach.

"Okay, then." Brea took a step back, dropping her hand. "Please come in." She stepped aside, shooing them all into the living room. "This is my home here in the human realm. I grew up here."

"Brea Robinson?" The President took slow measured steps into the overcrowded room. "I was told you lived here, yet you are not human?"

Brea raised her hand. "Changeling." She beamed a smile at the woman but didn't get a response. "Yes, I am fae. But I didn't know that until I was almost eighteen. Before that, I just thought I was crazy. Spent some time in a mental hospital to boot."

"I see." The President looked around, and Gulliver wondered if that was the only thing she could say.

"Please, come meet my daughter, the reigning Queen of Iskalt." Brea gestured to where Tia sat perched on the edge of her seat.

"Why are you no longer queen?" the President asked. "You are still young and surely more capable and mature for such an important role."

"Oh, I never wanted to be queen, though I was once heir to two kingdoms and married into a third, it was never my forte. My husband abdicated his throne when it became clear that Tia was ready. She was born to rule."

"And she's sitting right here, Mom. Stop talking about me

like I can't hear you." Tia hopped up from her seat and tried to hug the human president lady, but her guards were quick to step in. "Sorry, I'm just so excited to meet with the human ruler."

Tia returned to her seat, holding out a hand for the President to take the chair beside her.

The guards moved the chair to the opposite side of the room and put themselves between their ruler and the fae.

"All right." Tia smiled. "Whatever makes you most comfortable."

"I am not the ruler of all humans. I am the elected President of the United States of America. Though I speak for my people, I do not speak for the entire world."

"Yes, Mom said something about that."

"You'll have to forgive my high school knowledge of U.S. Politics." Brea shrugged. "My school years here were quite a long time ago."

"Tea! We need Tea. The water must be hot by now." Tia looked around for anyone capable of serving them. "Gullie?"

"On it." Gulliver grabbed Xavier by his shirt collar and hauled him into the kitchen.

"Can't you handle tea?" He pulled away.

"Not if you don't want me to blow up the kitchen."

"Excuse me?" One of the guards got a little too handsy with Gulliver. "What did you say?"

"He didn't mean it like that." Xavier came to his rescue. "He just meant he doesn't know how to run the tea kettle by himself." Xavier made a show of setting teacups onto a tray.

"Thanks." Gulliver brushed the creases out of his shirt. "They're a bit testy, aren't they?"

"Serving tea," Xavier muttered. "We should be in there talking peace."

"We're the lowest ranking fae in this house, even though

I'm a Lord. Everyone else is royalty. That means we get the tea." Gulliver placed tea bags into each of the cups and set the kettle onto the tray before carrying it into the living room. His hands trembled, and the teacups rattled on the tray as he set it in front of Tia.

"Oh dear, that's a dreadful-looking tea service."

"Sorry, Tia, that's all we had." Gulliver backed away as she poured hot water over the boring human tea bags.

"Sugar?" Tia asked the President, using the tongs to plop three or four cubes into her own teacup.

"Honey," the president replied absently. One of her guards took the cup and tasted it before passing it on to his queen.

Gulliver had a hard time thinking of her as anything other than the human queen when she acted more like one than any of the queens he knew, and he knew a lot of them.

President Worthington tapped a blunt fingernail against a chip in the teacup and frowned at their surroundings. "This is how a fae queen lives?"

"Not at all," Tia was quick to reply. "Not that we need all the finery and luxury of the Iskaltian palace. We do know how to live with little when we must. Should you come for a visit, we'd be happy to show you all of Iskalt, Fargelsi, and Eldur—"

"That won't be necessary." The President waved her hand to dismiss Tia's invitation. "We have much to discuss and not a great deal of time to discuss it." She set her tea aside, sat back against the worn upholstery of the chair, and crossed her legs. "I would end this struggle between the fae and humans within the borders of the United States."

"I would have it end everywhere," Tia added. "But first, we must come to some understanding."

"We cannot allow magic within our world. Humans cannot live under the threat of a power they do not possess."

"Magic is not a new thing in this world, Madame President," Brea said. "It has been here for many generations and has only now become widely known."

"My mother is right," Tia began. "Fae have been in your world for a very long time, and they have been suffering."

"Suffering?" The President sneered at the suggestion.

"Suffering," Tia insisted. "The Clarkson Institute and both the current Doctor Clarkson and his father, the senior Doctor Clarkson, have been behind HAFS since its inception decades ago."

President Worthington shook her head. "My intel tells me HAFS came together when the world went dark."

"That is when they came to the forefront of your media," Brea said.

"Are you aware that Doctor Clarkson has been conducting experiments on the fae living among you? And he has been for at least a generation?" Tia asked.

"What proof do you have?"

"I've seen it with my own eyes." Gulliver stepped forward. "I was in the institute just a few days ago to rescue my friend Sophie Devereaux—"

"The Sophie Devereaux who was abducted from her death bed in New Orleans? The daughter of HAFS Leader, Claude Devereaux?"

"Yes, ma'am." Gulliver bobbed his head. "She was taken there because HAFS believed that by taking her to the kingdom of Lenya and healing her of her illness, we somehow turned her into one of us."

"Which is not the case at all," Brea was quick to add.

"While we were there, we saw several Dark Fae locked in rooms. The doctor had somehow removed their defensive magic—the thing that hides our Dark Fae features when we are here in the human realm," Gulliver rambled. "It's the magic that makes you see me as human when, in reality, I have a very handsome tail and feline eyes that most humans would find alarming."

"A tail? You have a tail?"

"Yes, ma'am." Gulliver's tail swished behind him, but his defensive magic concealed its movement from her eyes. "I briefly met an Asrai in the institute, and her scales were bare for all to see. Even Sophie could see them."

"Scales?"

"Yes."

"Asrai are fae that most closely resemble the human mythological mermaids," Brea explained. "They have legs and arms, but they prefer the depths of the sea to land."

"I see," the President murmured.

"They experimented on Sophie," Gulliver went on. "She said it was incredibly painful. And her half-fae brother grew up there being experimented on. His magic is very erratic now because of Doctor Clarkson's meddling."

"HAFS has done a great deal of harm to my fae," Tia said in her most queenly voice. "It cannot continue. The violence you yourself have committed against the fae in your world cannot continue."

"I regret the actions we took against the fae in Los Angeles," President Worthington admitted. "At the time, it felt like the only possible action when that young man there claimed Los Angeles for the fae." She pointed across the room at Toby. "By taking the city, he declared war on the United States."

"My twin brother, Prince Tobias O'Shea did what he had to do to provide a safe place for the fae of this kingdom to take refuge."

"Country," Brea coughed.

"This country," Tia corrected before continuing. "He nor I saw that as an act of war, and I stand behind his decision. To my understanding, Los Angeles is only one city in your great nation. I would ask that you support our endeavors to make it a city for the fae and those who mean them no harm."

"I must protect my people." The President folded her hands in her lap. "No matter what, it is my responsibility to keep them safe from magic users."

Tia leaned forward with a small smile on her face. "That's just it. The fae of this world are my people, but they are also part human, which makes them yours as well. Collectively, it is our responsibility together to keep them safe. Just as I would protect my fae of Iskalt and you would protect your humans of the United States. Surely there must be a way we can come to an agreement that suits everyone involved."

"It's not about the people, your Majesty." The President seemed to shift her perspective as she gave Tia her undivided attention. As though she saw the young queen as her equal now. "It is about the magic they possess."

"One thing at a time, Madame President." Tia nodded. "We will come to an agreement on the use of magic within the human world. But first, we must agree to peace between our people."

"Perhaps." The President returned Tia's nod. "But we will need proof of the actions of Doctor Clarkson, and currently, he is missing."

"Oh, he is visiting my aunt's palace." Tia smiled. "He is perfectly safe and confined for the moment, but I will ask my uncle, Prince Griffin, and his son, Gulliver, to retrieve him for us while we continue our negotiations."

"I would very much like to speak with Doctor Clarkson. While we wait for his return, I will issue a warrant to search the institute for evidence of this experimentation. I am very eager to see what he's been up to."

Chapter Twenty-Three
SOPHIE

If Toby sat in that farmhouse for one moment longer, listening to that human queen speak as though the fae in her world meant nothing, he was going to do something they'd all regret. He paced across the kitchen, hanging on every word spoken in the living room.

The negotiations were mostly finished, and it was clear what the President wanted: an end to magic. She knew the fae of her realm weren't powerful wielders, but they weren't the ones she was worried about.

He should have left with Gullie and Griff to get Doctor Clarkson, but Tia hadn't let him. Now, he stared at President Worthington.

"You can't be serious." His voice was louder than he'd intended, but he didn't back down. "That's ... that's ..."

"Not a bad solution," Tia finished, though she knew very well it wasn't what her brother thought at all. The look she sent him said as much.

He shot across the room, and one of the guards in black blocked his path.

"Chillax, man." Toby stepped sideways to avoid bumping into him. "I won't hurt your queen. I just need some air."

As he hurried outside, he heard Lochlan ask Brea what in all the magic his son meant by chillax.

Even his father's disdain for stupid human words couldn't stop the ringing in his ears, the howling of his thoughts.

The President of this human kingdom wanted to close off the fae world, to prevent fae from traveling through portals to reach their lands. Was it possible?

If it was, how could they even entertain such an idea? The O'Shea magic was part of the very fabric of fae life. They may not particularly like the humans, but it didn't change the fact they were connected to them, to their world.

Toby reached the overgrown front lawn that had provided a somewhat-soft landing spot for portal travelers since he was a kid clinging to his father's arm.

He hadn't realized his legs gave out until they hit the hard earth. There was no pain in them, only a sharp ache right in the center of his chest.

His power, the only magic he had, was considered by humans to be the most dangerous threat to their well-being.

A breeze rustled through his hair, cooling the day's heat. Dusk would be upon them soon, the moon rising into the sky to remind Toby he wasn't useless. There was some purpose for him in one of these worlds.

But what if that went away?

What if it all ended? Without the ability to open portals, who was he?

"Is it possible?" a soft voice asked behind him.

Toby didn't respond to Xavier's question right away. His harsh laughter drifted into the cloudy sky. "Possible? With magic, there are nearly no limitations."

That was what scared him.

What the President asked for ... could most likely be done. They only had to find the way.

He closed his eyes, feeling for the thinness of the veil that existed right here. The portals damaged that wall between worlds, but he'd never truly considered it damage. It brought the humans and fae closer together.

Now, they would be driven further apart.

Xavier extended a hand down to him, but Toby didn't take it. He couldn't go back into that room where his sister negotiated away their ancestral right.

A sigh hissed out of Xavier, and he lowered himself to the grass in front of Toby. "You're scared."

"I'm not." He'd gone through too much in his life to fear losing the ability that caused so much of that strife. If it wasn't for his O'Shea magic, Egan wouldn't have taken him. The human wars would have stayed just that ... human.

Except, when he considered the idea that he could lose the one thing that made him valuable to any of the royals he considered family, it made him need to hit something.

He pulled at the grass, yanking it with such force it ripped out in clumps.

Xavier didn't stop him. Instead, he began pulling the tall grasses right alongside him until they were both too tired to continue. Yet, Toby couldn't stop. He needed to let out every ounce of energy his body possessed.

"Toby."

He could hardly hear him.

"Tobes."

His fingers ached as he clawed at the dirt, not so different from the ground underneath his own palace.

There was pressure on his arm before warmth blew across his lips. Xavier closed the gap between them, stopping Toby's frantic movements by freezing him in place with a kiss.

His lips were thick, warm. And for once, Toby didn't think. He let his mind go blank and the moment take over. Energy flooded his limbs, but it was more than that.

"You are more than your magic, Tobias O'Shea," Xavier whispered.

Toby pulled back. "What was that for?"

One corner of Xavier's mouth tipped up. "Sometimes, a guy has to make a moment what he wishes it to be and not what it is."

Toby gingerly touched his lips. Sure, Xavier only wanted to calm him down, to take away the panic, but he could do it that way anytime.

For the first time since Logan died, Toby wanted to be here, to continue in this life that his first love didn't get to see. Even if it meant losing part of himself in the process.

Toby curled his fingers into Xavier's shirt and yanked him forward for another bolstering kiss before shoving him back. "Tell Tia I've gone to get answers."

"Tobes—"

"No, I'm okay. I swear. But there's someone I need to speak with."

As the only fae in known history to travel by portal from one fae kingdom to the next without a stop in the human realm, maybe the solution didn't have to be giving up his power entirely. Only part of it.

He was gone before Xavier could stop him, snapping the

portal shut to avoid having any followers. This was an answer he had to find without Xavier, as much as he wanted him by his side.

The moment he set foot outside Radur City, he hurried toward the somewhat-repaired pillars of Aghadoon. There was still a lot of work to do before they could attempt moving the village again, but it was coming along.

It was just past dawn in Eldur, and the day's heat was only beginning. The streets of Aghadoon had been repaired with new masonry, the brick layers working long hours. Yet, they were abandoned at the moment.

He wandered the silent village on his way to the library, but when he got there, the door was locked. Only his grandfather had the ability to open the sealed magic, but when he was awake, he always left it open.

Toby sat with his back against the door, waiting. He'd wait all day if he had to.

Lucky for him, it wasn't long before the door opened, sending him sprawling into the library.

"Thanks," he grumbled, rubbing his head where it hit the floor. "A warning would have been nice."

"Where's the fun in that?" Brandon smiled down at him. "If you're here, Toby, and not in the human realm with their queen, there must be a reason. Come. I'll send for some Eldur brew."

"Please don't. You're as bad as Mom."

He stepped over Toby and into the library. "I've developed quite a taste for the stuff. It certainly provides an energy tea cannot."

"As if you or Mom need that." His grandfather was tireless.

"Stop with that attitude, boy." Grandfather Brandon gave a disapproving frown. "You sound like your sister. Go on, get up and come tell me what has you worried."

Toby sighed as he climbed to his feet and closed the door behind him. He sank into a chair at the long wooden table. Around him, scrolls appeared and disappeared from shelves that almost seemed to shake each time. It wasn't a place one got used to, but the familiarity was nice. The library somehow knew what it was a fae needed to know and searched its deep wells of information for anything that could be of help.

Brandon picked up a scroll from the shelf nearest him and unrolled it, his dark brows pinching together on his seemingly young face. "Ah, the veil."

"The humans want it repaired and sealed."

"Haven't we attempted that before?"

He wasn't wrong. When Egan tore through the veil in Myrkur, they did everything to try to fix it, but in the end, they just sent Griff and Riona to guard the rift.

"That was different." At least, he hoped so. "We wanted to seal just one area. Mom said it was like spot treating a carpet that was fully covered in wine stains."

Brandon rubbed the back of his neck, his lips pursed. It was an expression almost entirely reserved for Brea and her human tendencies. "I ... what?"

"She says the veil has too much damage to only heal one part of it without causing further weakness. We think we cause it to thin every time we travel into the human realm."

"Interesting." His eyes sparked with curiosity. "So, in order to heal each weak point, we need to wash the entire thing?"

How did a man who rarely left Aghadoon understand Toby's mother's analogy more than he did? "I guess."

The pensive look on his face was dangerous, and Toby knew what was coming as the man took a seat across from him. "Do you know what this means?"

"Of course I do." Toby hadn't meant to snap, but his emotions were so heightened he almost couldn't control him.

"Sorry, Grandfather." He needed another of Xavier's kisses to calm the panic welling in his chest.

Brandon waved off the insult. "Boy, if I took offense every time someone sassed me, I'd have thrown your sister off the highest point in Iskalt long ago.'

Toby bit back a smile. He'd give anything for things to be like they once were. Before Tia took the throne, she'd have been right at his side searching scrolls and books for any way to save their family's legacy.

She had bigger responsibilities now, and he'd accepted that the moment his father set the crown on her head.

"Start with this one." Brandon slid a book across the table. "It is tales of the portal magic throughout the generations before your father was born."

The book was fascinating, and Toby wished he'd thought to research his power before now, but it held none of the answers he sought. He flipped through it, looking for shreds of information about the veil.

Next, it was a scroll that looked like it had been pulled right from the flames.

"What does this say?" He pointed to a line in Fargelsi, a language he'd never mastered.

Brandon smiled. "The blessed will rule the fae."

"Blessed ..."

"There was a time when Fargelsians thought the O'Shea magic was all that kept our world from falling apart. It's not typically believed now, but hundreds of years ago, they needed something to hold on to, even if it was a power that originated in another kingdom."

He pushed that scroll aside and began another. Then another. Book after book, scroll after scroll.

The daylight came and went. Fae brought them Eldur brew

and sustenance. Toby drank the brew without tasting it, smelling it. All he cared about was that it kept him alert.

Brandon offered him a room for the night, but he chose to sleep in the library so he could wake early and begin the process again.

The magic of the library showed him everything he would ever need to know about the O'Shea magic and its history, about the veil and how it came to be.

He wasn't sure how late it was when a line caught his eye. He leaned forward and pulled a small oil lantern closer to the thick book.

There it was. The beginning of his answer.

A way to end this war with the humans.

When the door opened, spilling moonlight across the threshold, Brandon stepped in. "I think you need a break, Toby."

Toby shook his head, his eyes lifting in the glow of the lantern. "I know what we have to do."

Chapter Twenty-Four
GULLIVER

Well, that was interesting. Gulliver couldn't stop thinking of the disdain the President had for Doctor Clarkson when she looked at him that first time.

Maybe, just maybe she didn't truly hate the fae.

"What just happened?" Griff was the first person to voice what they were all wondering.

It took more than a day to retrieve the doctor, so the negotiations with the President lasted a second day. When she returned that time, they'd been more prepared.

Now, she was gone, leaving behind a group of stunned fae and half-fae.

Sophie shrugged. "I think she's been getting some very bad advice."

"What?" Brea asked.

"It's obvious she wants to do the right thing, despite her aloofness. "I voted for her, to the dismay of my father. She's our first female president and has a lot of pressure on her, but she's always seemed genuine. The battle of Aghadoon will always stain her presidency, but I don't think it was entirely her call."

Tia had been quiet since the President's departure, and Gulliver watched her, trying to gauge what she thought. "I need to talk to Kier." She sighed. "He's much better at reading people than me. He should be here and not in Iskalt."

Lochlan put a hand on her shoulder. "Someone had to run the kingdom. Don't discount yourself. You agreed to this meeting because you sensed it could do some good."

"But has it? Can we even do what she wants? Do we want to?"

"Are you serious right now?" Orla rose to her full height. "You can't really be considering not following through. This is a road to peace, to living in safety."

"You don't understand." Gulliver couldn't help speaking up. "Traveling between realms ... our connection to humans, they're asking us to give it up."

"So?" Sophie scowled at him. "The humans wish for you to give up one tiny freedom in order to save countless lives. Are you fae really this selfish?"

"Don't you speak to him that way, human." Tia jumped between Sophie and Gulliver. "Not after everything he's done for you."

"Can we all just calm down?" Brea asked.

They ignored her.

"I just don't understand," Sophie said. "What is there to think about? The half-fae and human sympathizer lives in this realm mean more than your ability to get a cheeseburger every once in a while."

Gulliver thought of all the times they'd used traveling through the veil for necessary means. Stopping Eagan. Finding the means to free everyone trapped in Myrkur. Saving Sophie in Lenya. Speedy travel to another fae kingdom. They'd saved lives, changed their world.

Inter-realm travel was so much a part of their world it was hard to imagine society without it.

Yet, all he could manage to say was, "I *really* like tacos."

That broke the tension in the room, a tension born of tough decisions like allowing the humans to take Doctor Clarkson into custody as a show of good faith. Like agreeing to seal the veil.

Tia's arm slipped around his waist. "Gul, I need you to go help Toby. Griff can take you. We all need to get out of the human realm, but I should go to Iskalt and consult with Kier. I'll search the archives there for anything that might be helpful."

As much as he wanted to be part of this decision, it wasn't his to make and he couldn't deny Tia anything. Silently, he nodded.

Sophie followed him out. "I'm sorry."

"I know." He pushed out a breath and lifted his face to the stars. One day, maybe night would only be for sleeping and not traveling through realms.

"I just don't understand how it's even something you all need to think about. Traveling through the human realm, bringing fae here, has brought you nothing but pain."

She was wrong but he couldn't voice why. Maybe he should have seen it that way too, but instead, the vision in his mind was crowding onto the couch with Tia and Toby to watch

Netflix. Raiding the kitchen or devouring a pizza while laughing and telling stories.

Some of the best parts of their lives happened here.

He looked back over his shoulder to where Brea sat on the front steps surveying the grounds. Could she really agree to never again set foot in her first home?

Sophie's hand slid into his moments before Griff burst through the front door. The screen slammed shut behind him. He leaned down to say something to Brea, making her laugh.

"You're right." Gulliver squeezed her hand. "We all know you are. There is nothing more important than ending this conflict."

"I know what they're asking of you isn't easy."

They weren't only asking it of him. Sophie may not have realized it yet, but without the portals, they may never see each other again. He looked away to hide the tears in his eyes. No human would choose a world not their own unless they were Myles Merrick.

"Time to go, Gul." Griff approached with a bounce in his step that shouldn't have been there. He was an O'Shea. The ability to cross the veil was his birthright, and he was going to lose it.

"You coming, Sophie?" Griff asked.

She shook her head. It was only a precursor of the real decision that was to come. The sudden thought hit Gullie that this could be it. Would he come back before the portal was closed?

"I ..." He couldn't get the words out. *Goodbye. I don't want to leave you.*

Sophie put a hand on each side of his face, her thumbs tracing the tops of his cheekbones. "Hey ... it's okay."

"But what if—"

She kissed him, slowly this time. He didn't know what it meant, if she was trying to remember him.

"I'll make it back before the veil closes," he whispered against her lips. He had to. This couldn't be it.

Griff cleared his throat, and Gulliver pulled away, his face heating.

Sophie offered him one final smile, and he burned the image into his mind as he stepped into the gateway to Eldur and the scene faded away.

Gulliver was so used to his father's portals he barely noticed it until he slammed into the ground outside Aghadoon. His knees rattled, but he managed to stay on his feet.

"Always improving." Griff grinned.

Gulliver ignored him, heading straight for the village that now held too many nightmares. He tried not to see the vacant eyes of rebels who'd tried to fight the combined forces of HAFS and the kingdom of the United States. He tried to shrug off the chill being back here caused.

There were no choices anymore. Maybe there never had been.

He found the door to the library open, but he hadn't expected anything else. Unlike his sister, Toby had been an early riser even before Logan died. He had normally gone through the paces of a sparring workout and handled some of his princely duties before she slinked down for breakfast.

Except this time, the alertness from his eyes was gone.

"What's wrong with him?" Griff whispered, worry edging his words.

Gulliver approached slowly, rounding the table to look into Toby's dazed eyes as he hunched over a book. He grabbed the book to see what it was, but Toby snatched it back.

"I can't get him to sleep." Brandon entered, carrying a tray. "He's living on a diet of Eldur brew and cheese."

"Toby hates Eldur brew." Something was seriously wrong.

Brandon shrugged and leaned down to set the tray on the

table. "Tobes, you have company."

"I know." He grunted and continued reading.

"What book is that?" Griff asked.

"I'm not sure." Brandon's brow creased. "It's not the one I left him with when I went to bed last night, but once you know what you're looking for, the library chooses the books."

Griff gestured to the door. "Why don't you show me some of the repairs."

Both men gave Gulliver a look, and he knew their repair inspection was just an excuse to leave him alone with his friend.

"Thanks," he murmured. It was all on him.

If they were to have peace with the humans, the library had to show Toby what he needed to know, and Gulliver needed to get that out of him.

He pulled out the chair beside Toby, the wooden legs scraping against the stone floor. "Hi." He sat.

"Not now, Gullie."

Gulliver nodded, folding his hands in his lap. "I can wait."

"Are you just going to stare at me?"

"Yes."

A growl ripped from his throat, but the hazy quality of his eyes cleared as he finally looked up. "We were never supposed to have this power."

"What?"

Toby's entire body quaked. "This ... the library has shown me things. Ancient scrolls that look like they haven't been opened since they were written hundreds of years ago. A book with crumbling pages."

"Toby?"

"The O'Shea magic ... it was created to destroy the veil between worlds." Toby's voice held only a hint of the agony he was likely feeling at such a revelation.

Silence was Gulliver's only response. There were no words that could accurately describe the dread churning inside him.

Toby pushed a hand roughly through his hair. "Darragh O'Shea, my distant ancestor, he wanted to destroy the veil. A weakness in a certain location allowed him to access the human realm, a rift similar to that in Myrkur. It showed him another creature not unlike us, except in one thing. They didn't have magic. They were powerless against us. Weak creatures easily controlled."

He paused, scrubbing a hand over his face. "The humans are right to fear us. This magic I've been clinging to only had one purpose: to rip through the veil and allow the fae to control both realms. Power. That's what it always comes down to, isn't it? More power."

"But they didn't." Gulliver leaned on the table, hardly able to hold himself up. "The veil still exists."

"Because the magic he created wasn't powerful enough for the task. Each generation it's thought to have grown. He knew that one day, there would be an O'Shea capable of his goals."

"There hasn't been—" Gulliver stopped, his eyes widening.

"An O'Shea with the portal magic of two," Toby said softly.

Tia's O'Shea power was erratic, weak. With her other magic, Toby was her amplifier. What if—

"Me."

Tia's weakness made him stronger, just like his bolstered her.

"The library showed you this?" Gulliver prayed he was wrong, that there was another explanation for why the veil weakened so much at the points Toby traveled through.

Toby slid a book in front of Gulliver. "That's not everything."

"I don't read Fargelsian."

"Concentrate. There's only a few lines here or there I can't read, and the entire realm knows I couldn't speak Fargelsian if I was on fire and their words would put it out."

"*Kaefa*."

"Need a handkerchief?"

"No, I mean that's the word you'd use to put out the fire." Gulliver knew a few basics, but beyond that, he was lost.

"Just read." Toby tapped the book.

Gulliver focused on the words until the letters swam before him, rearranging into recognizable words. "What the ..." He didn't finish the phrase because his gaze caught on a line of text that had translated to, 'All rifts in the veil must be healed to prevent it from splitting'.

He lifted his eyes.

Toby nodded. "We risk it every time we travel. Even more so when we use my portals. I don't think we're at the point yet where it's on the verge of collapsing, but we could get there soon. Especially with my power."

Gulliver continued reading, each line getting worse than the one before it. When he reached the part that must have turned Toby into the mess he was, he inhaled a sharp rush of air. "No."

Toby nodded, burying his face in his hands. "How am I going to tell Tia? My father? Your father?"

Gulliver didn't know. He reached over, pulling Toby sideways into a hug as his friend's world crashed.

Not only did they have to seal the veil entirely, but the only way to do that was to destroy what they held most dear.

Portal magic.

The O'Shea right by birth.

They couldn't just fix what they'd broken and promise not to break it again.

Their magic had to be destroyed entirely.

Chapter Twenty-Five

SOPHIE

"You want to take me to New Orleans through a portal?" Sophie blinked at Gulliver, trying to focus on his words and not on her relief at seeing him again. "The same portals that are ripping holes in the veil?"

He couldn't be that dim.

"It's faster and we're working on a way to repair the veil." Gulliver planted his feet as though preparing to argue with her for as long as it took.

"I don't want to contribute to the problem." She gave him her most stubborn look, equally ready to strengthen her point.

"It's not going to be a problem for much longer."

"I'll take a bus. It will be fine. I just need someone to watch

Noah while I'm gone."

"We'll both go with you. My dad can stay with Noah while you and I go do whatever it is you have to do."

"I'm going to see my father alone." She jutted her chin out in defiance. She had a plan, and she would see it through.

"It's not safe to see him alone, Sophie." Gulliver's voice softened with sympathy. "He's still heavily involved with HAFS."

She nodded. "And he killed my mother for her involvement with the fae, and he planned to do the same to me. I have things to say to him. In private."

"At least let me go with you to the house. I'll wait outside in the sweltering heat by myself."

She threw her hands up in the air. "Fine. But we're leaving now. I already bought us bus tickets."

"Us, us? Or us, as in you and Noah?"

"I don't want him anywhere near my father. But I figured you would insist on coming with me." She was secretly glad he wanted to come. She didn't want to miss any time she had left with him.

"Dad will take good care of Noah." Gulliver nodded, as if it was all settled.

"Dad will do what now?" Griffin shuffled into the kitchen at the farmhouse, where there was no such thing as a private conversation.

"Watch Noah while we go to New Orleans so I can speak with my father." Sophie crossed her arms over her chest.

Griffin studied her for a moment and must have seen her resolve. "All right. He can go back with me to Eldur for a few days."

"Must you travel by portal?" Sophie twisted her hands together. "I hate to further contribute to the damage to the veil. Could you stay here with him?"

"I need to be in Aghadoon, and we have a lot of fae who will need to come back to the human realm before this is over. I promise, we will find a way to heal the damage done to the veil."

"Okay." Sophie nodded. "But we're taking a bus to New Orleans."

"You two need to hurry back here. Our time in this world is coming to an end, and we have to be ready to go home once the peace is settled."

"I'll be back as soon as I can," Gulliver said.

Sophie didn't want to think about the long trip back, knowing the hardest goodbye she would ever have to face loomed ahead of her.

"Take Brea's plastic money card." Griffin fished the card from his back pocket. "And trade those bus tickets in for airfare. It's nearly as fast as a portal."

"What? No! I don't like flying. If I was meant to fly, I'd have wings like Mom's. But I don't. I have a tail. And my tail and I would rather stay on the ground."

"You're afraid of an airplane, but you'll willingly step into a magic portal like it's nothing?" Sophie tried to hide her smile.

"As long as it's not Tia's portal, then yes." Gulliver clutched something to his chest. Something she couldn't quite see, but she knew it was his tail.

"It would be faster if we could fly." She cast her eyes down with a small smile just for him.

Gullie heaved a sigh. "Fine. But I don't like it."

He took the credit card from Griffin.

"Why do you have Brea's human money card?" Gulliver wore a bemused smile.

"I borrowed it to pay for cheeseburgers. She won't care if you use it to help Sophie."

"Thanks, Dad. And by that, I mean, thank Brea for me." Gullie ran upstairs to gather his things for the trip.

Sophie went to tell Noah goodbye, promising she would come get him in Eldur when it was safe. She tried to hide the smile on her face, knowing she would get to see the fae world one last time before the veil closed forever.

"Does it ever cool off in this city?" Gulliver wiped his brow as they left the airport terminal. He hated the airports almost as much as the airplane. Sophie tried not to laugh at the memory of his hand wrapped around hers as the plane took off and again when it landed.

"Not much." Sophie soaked in the NOLA atmosphere, knowing she would likely never see it again after this trip. She couldn't live in the same city as her father. She had a responsibility to keep Noah safe, and as long as Claude Devereaux had a vendetta against the fae, he would pose a threat against Noah. "But it's home and I've always loved it here."

She gazed across the line of waiting Ubers for the one she'd ordered when they landed.

"This way." She ducked into the backseat of a bright red SUV.

"You sure?" Gulliver hesitated. "It's easier than you think to accidentally get in the wrong car."

"I'm sure." She giggled at the look on his face, remembering the story he'd told her of accidentally abducting a lady thinking she drove a taxi.

"You going to the Quarter, ma'am?" the Uber driver confirmed.

"Yes, you can just drop us off at the corner of Esplanade and Burgundy."

Gulliver clutched the door handle, and his eyes shifted uneasily as they left the airport behind.

"You okay?"

"Sorry, I'm always a little uneasy with human drivers I don't know."

"Human?" The driver glanced in his rearview mirror. "You one of those fae people?"

"Nope." Gulliver shook his head furiously. "Not me, dude."

"Aw, that's too bad. Always wanted to meet a fae. The haters give them a bad rap, but I think they're kind of cool."

Gulliver's ears turned red, and Sophie could only imagine the way the very tips of his ears would look in the fae realm. Here, he looked very much human. Handsome, though not quite himself.

The driver dropped them off just a block from the house where Sophie grew up.

"You okay, Sophie?" Gulliver grabbed her arm and tugged her close.

"Not really, why?" Her voice trembled.

"You're awfully pale."

"I'm just nervous. I'll be okay."

They walked along Esplanade Avenue, and Sophie recalled some of her earliest memories walking this same path with her mother. She couldn't help but think her mom could have saved them all a lot of heartache if she hadn't fallen in love with a fae and had a child with him. In a way, she couldn't fault her father for being angry. But she would never forgive him for killing her mother. She held him responsible for everything that had happened to Noah after that horrible night when he was ripped from her arms and taken from his fae father. She had no idea what happened to Noah's father, and she might never know, but before this day was out, Claude Devereaux would no longer have a daughter.

"Are you sure you want me to stay out here?" Gulliver held her hand tightly in his. "I can come with you for moral support."

"Thanks, Gullie, but I need to do this on my own. I won't be long." She reached for the iron gate that led to her backyard. To the garden that had once been her haven from the rest of the world. She paused for a moment as memories of her father drifted through her mind in a flash. "How could a man who loved me so much be capable of such cruelty?"

"He let hate into his heart, but he always loved you. Don't let him rob you of your happy memories."

She nodded. "Wait here."

He squeezed her hand one last time before he let go, and she stepped through the gate to find her father working in her mother's garden. The sight used to make her smile. The way he lovingly tended the flowers her mother had cultivated. She used to think he did it to keep her memory alive for Sophie. But now, as she watched him, she saw the guilt weighing heavily on his shoulders.

"Dad," she whispered.

"Sophie?" Claude leapt to his feet, letting his eyes scan the grounds, looking for HAFS members. "You shouldn't be here." He jogged across the expanse of lawn that separated them, his work overalls hanging on his frame. A testament to the weight he'd lost quickly in recent weeks.

"I won't stay long." She moved to sit under the umbrella on the patio where they'd shared in countless memories.

"They said you escaped. That you killed the doctor."

Sophie snorted at that. "I didn't kill anyone. Doctor Clarkson is in U.S. custody now, waiting to stand trial for his crimes."

"Crimes?"

"Against the fae he experimented on in his house of horrors. The institute you subjected me to."

"Fae are not human. You cannot commit a crime against them."

"Is that what you tell yourself at night to make you feel better about the choices you've made?"

"They've manipulated you, honey." He sank into the wrought iron seat beside her.

"Just like they did my mother?" Sophie stared at him. "Is that why you killed her? Because you thought she had been manipulated?"

"I tried to get through to her. I tried so hard to bring her back."

"She didn't want to be with you, Dad. That was her biggest crime. She fell in love with someone else, and you couldn't deal with it, so you killed her for it and sent her son to the institute, where Clarkson performed perverse experiments on him. The poor boy never received a name. Never got to play outside in the sun. Never breathed fresh air. You did that to him. To my brother."

"He's not your brother!" Claude brought his fist down on the chair arm. "He is fae filth."

"He is part human. Part of *Mom*. All the fae of this world are mostly human. Yet, you and all your friends would condemn them for the drops of fae blood in their veins. Just because your wife chose to be with one of them instead of you."

"Shut up!" Spittle flew from his mouth, and his eyes widened in crazed anger.

"Will you kill me now too? Because I don't think the way you do? Because I've fallen in love with a fae too?"

"Sophie." His voice broke, and all the fight went out of him. "I could never harm you."

"But you turned me over to Clarkson knowing full well what he would do to me. That if given the chance, he would kill me if I proved useless to his experimentation."

"I had to let them take you. It was the only way to get you back."

"That's your problem." Sophie stood. "You hold on to the people you love so tightly that you suffocate them. You force them to your will." She let out a mirthless laugh. "You forced me to take treatments when I would have rather died. And then, when I was healed, you forced me into an institute where they tried to rip the magic from my veins. The very magic that healed me."

"I just wanted you to be safe and healthy." A whine entered Claude's voice.

"Well, you got your wish. Just not how you wanted. I am safe and healthy, but my priorities have changed now. For the rest of my life, I will think only of my brother and his happiness. I will do whatever it takes to keep him safe."

"Wait." He reached for her. "Let me explain."

"You have." She shrugged. "You did everything you could to keep me safe within the web of lies you built up around me. To keep the truth from me so in my ignorance, I would love you. But you didn't have to make the choices you made. You didn't have to kill my mother just because she wanted to leave you. You could have let her go. You could have moved on and everything would have been different. But you didn't. And now you will pay the consequences. No matter what happens from here, you will never see me again." She started to walk away.

"No, please. You have to forgive me." Claude grasped onto her hand, dropping to his knees beside her.

"I have, Dad. I can forgive you for all the lies and the way you kept me sheltered from the truth. I can even forgive you for your willful ignorance against the fae. I just can't forgive you for killing our mother." She tugged her hand away and he let her go.

"Where will you go?"

"I don't know, but it won't be here."

Chapter Twenty-Six
TOBY

"Are you sure we have to do this?" It wasn't the first time Tia asked what each of them were thinking. Did they really have to give up such a large part of their family's identity to keep their fae safe?

Toby slid his hand into hers. They sat in the Aghadoon courtyard, the very same one that had bombs raining down on it not long ago. "I wish there was another way."

On the bench beside them, Lochlan and Griff were silent. This was their legacy too, and yet, they'd decided it was up to the twins, the very fae who'd caused the weakness in the veil if the texts were to be believed.

And they were. They always were.

Nothing that came out of the Aghadoon library held falsehoods. Hidden truths, yes, but not blatant lies. It was the only knowledge that could truly be trusted.

Tia leaned her head on their father's shoulder. "Do you ever think how much better off the fae worlds would be without anyone as powerful as me and Tobes?"

He waited a beat before responding. "Different, maybe." His hand lifted to skim over the side of her head. "But not better off. Never better off."

Griff nodded in agreement. "Without you, I'd still be in that prison realm ... if Egan hadn't found a way to take over each kingdom by now."

"Keir would probably be dead," Toby put in.

His father shot him a disapproving look, one he didn't understand.

"What? It's true. All of Lenya would have been consumed by the fire plains if she hadn't messed up her portal and dropped into Keir's lap."

Tia sighed. "I guess time is up on learning how to properly control the O'Shea power."

Toby snorted. "You were never going to win that battle, T."

Griff, seated on Toby's other side, slapped him on the back of the head. "What is wrong with you, kid?"

What was wrong with him? They were about to seal off the human realm, stripping him of his only magic and preventing him from seeing any of his new friends who decided to stay there. They still didn't know if the half-fae would ever truly be safe. "Many, many things."

Lochlan sighed, a knowing quality to it. He always seemed to sense his children's problems, but he believed in letting them come to him, unlike Brea, who wanted to charge right in and fix everything.

This time, she couldn't.

"Do you remember the first time we went through a portal?" Tia asked, lifting her head to peer at Toby.

One corner of his mouth rose. That was a day he'd never forget. "Mom's birthday."

They'd been seven years old. His mother claimed she refused to take them to the human realm until they were old enough to remember it because everyone should remember their first time.

"Dad got her an ice cream cake."

Mom's favorite—ice cream. One of the more ridiculous human creations he'd miss. Uncle Myles had been there with his human family. Even Alona came through the veil, and she didn't like to visit the world that should have been hers.

Tears hung in Tia's lashes, and Toby hated that he couldn't do anything to rid her of them.

"This is the right thing." She closed her eyes.

Each of the other O'Sheas nodded.

She sniffed. "Then, why does it hurt so much? What does our family have after this? What makes us special?"

After a long silence, it was their father who answered. "Our family has us. We were never meant to wield this power. It was created to cause havoc. So, when you ask what we have, the answer will be peace. That's worth every ounce of magic the fae world possesses."

Xavier approached slowly, as if he didn't know if he was welcome. Toby stood to greet him. "Is it time?"

He looked to the darkening sky, where the stars felt absent on a night like this.

Xavier nodded. "We can't wait any longer."

Toby knew Tia wanted to come along, to have one last human adventure, but this wasn't the time. She was still the Queen of Iskalt. Keir would arrive in the morning, and she had to be here to receive his report on her kingdom.

"Be safe, son." Lochlan touched his arm.

Griff sent him a grim smile. "You were meant for this."

They didn't know what they'd find in Los Angeles. The President promised to begin setting it up as a sanctuary city for anyone with fae blood, but that meant half-fae congregating in the open where HAFS could find them. Would they be building high walls to keep the fae in? Patrolling them with their terrifying human weapons?

"Do we have any news?" he asked Xavier as they headed for Aghadoon's front gate.

Xavier nodded. "All indications point to the humans holding up their end of the bargain. For now."

Toby couldn't help smiling.

"What?" Xavier elbowed him.

"Nothing."

"Tobes, we're about to head into magic knows what and you're smiling."

"It's just ... you're sounding more like a fae. You called them humans instead of us."

"Well ..." He rubbed the back of his neck. "When they treat you like an other, you feel like one. We aren't fae, but we're not fully human either. Our community is in a bit of an identity crisis right now."

Toby understood every word. His entire life had been one giant identity crises. "I'm an other too, I guess."

Xavier looped their arms together. "I'm starting to wonder if everyone is."

Toby was still thinking about his words when they met Orla and a handful of her most trusted fighters on the outskirts of Radur City.

"Do we know how many there will be?" he asked.

Orla shrugged. "I'm guessing quite a few. Our people have

been attacked and threatened. Many won't want to stay in the human realm."

The four queens of the fae—and King Hector—offered asylum to any half-fae who wished to leave the human realm. Once the veil was healed and sealed, they'd stay on this side and begin a new life, one they could never have imagined.

"And the call went out?"

"Yes." Orla clasped her hands behind her back. "I sent the message around the world through our network. We've given them a week now. All half-fae or fae living in the human realm who wish to leave must make it to L.A. They'll be there."

The President's aides helped them find a venue to meet. It was in the human leader's best interest to encourage the fae to leave her lands.

A heaviness settled in Toby's chest at the thought of disconnecting from the community who'd stay, disconnecting from Xavier. It was like cleaving the new world he'd found in two. He kept asking the heavens what Logan would do, but this time, he received no answer.

Logan wasn't here, but Toby was.

"Okay, let's get going." Hands grasped for him, not wanting to break contact as he pulled the power from the depths of himself. It set him alight, made every part of him come alive.

He'd miss this feeling.

Moving into the light, he brought the others along, not even straining to hold the portal together. It wasn't supposed to be this easy. He knew that. Maybe it should have been a sign that he held too much power.

His concentration broke as they tumbled toward an L.A. street outside the half-fae headquarters. The pavement came up to meet him, and he rolled as he crashed into it, popping back up to his feet.

The others moaned from where they'd collapsed onto the road.

Behind them, a door opened and an unfamiliar man stuck his head out. "Thank the great Lord above." He was older with salt and pepper hair and a weathered face. He quickly went to Orla and helped her to her feet. "Y'all gave us a fright. We've been waiting."

Orla dusted herself off and started moving.

"We're here now, Robinson." She strode past him into the warehouse.

Robinson.

"Is that a first name or last?" he asked Xavier.

Xavier's wince told him everything he needed to know. He tried to walk ahead, but Toby yanked him back. "The man who raised my mother, a human, is working for you?"

Jack Robinson wasn't his grandfather. He refused to think of him as such after the stories he'd heard. The man was the reason Toby's mom ended up at the Clarkson Institute.

"Careful." Xavier looked around and dropped his voice. "He joined us after his wife was killed in a HAFS bombing."

"Why didn't you tell me?"

"Not every piece of information will help, Toby. Some only make what we have to do harder." Like working with the man who neglected Brea, allowed HAFS to have her, and then told HAFS she was dead, so they didn't keep searching for her. It was hard to separate the actions.

Xavier looked at the device on his wrist. "We need to be at the arena in an hour."

He'd called it the Staples Center, but that just sounded like random sounds put together. The President's people had apparently made a call to secure the location and provide security assistance if needed.

Jack was speaking when Toby and Xavier joined the others.

"We've received government funds to transform derelict housing to suit our needs with half-fae pouring in from around the globe. The mayor has called three times and wishes to have a meeting with you, Orla." He looked down at a list he was reading. "The protestors have been out there night and day, but so far, they haven't been violent. Some of them raise guns in the air, but they do not shoot."

"HAFS must be waiting for something." Orla bent over an inside view of the arena. "Is everything in place?"

He nodded.

She straightened. "Good. Then, we cannot wait any longer. Xavier, pull a car around back. Robinson, you're staying here."

Xavier jogged off to obey her, leaving Toby to study the warehouse. A wall of screens sat at one end with a woman behind them, typing furiously on a keyboard.

There were half-fae rushing past and even a few humans. It was like the center of the half-fae universe.

One of Orla's men opened the door for them, and they walked into the alley to find Xavier behind the wheel of a shiny yellow car. "Taxi anyone?" he asked.

Toby knew it! He'd have to tell Gulliver. They weren't wrong about the yellow cars.

It was a short drive through mostly deserted streets. Xavier had told him of humans packing up and leaving their homes. Some stayed, but the city had emptied considerably. For now. Soon, it would be teeming with half-fae.

When they stopped, a giant domed building loomed over them.

"This is a staple?" he asked.

Xavier looked sideways at him, one eyebrow lifted. "Just ... sure, Tobes." He gave him a strange look and chuckled to himself. This is what a staple looks like."

Everything looked even bigger inside. High ceilings, a long

pathway that seemed to go around in a circle. Xavier led him to an opening in the wall, and he froze. Before him stood a massive room, probably the biggest he'd ever seen. Wooden floors, odd devices hanging from the ceiling. Thousands of chairs.

And not a single half-fae.

Orla looked just as confused as he felt. "Xavier, the message we sent had clear instructions, correct?"

"I thought so."

"Well, we have to wait." They didn't have long, but the half-fae who wanted out would come. They lowered themselves into folding seats, and no one said a word.

They'd expected hundreds, maybe thousands. The fae realm was safe for them, something they couldn't one hundred percent guarantee of the human realm.

Yet, the emptiness echoed.

Footsteps sounded on the steps behind them, and Toby looked up to find a man and a woman.

The woman smiled as she approached, and he stood. "Hello, I'm Prince Tobias. You're safe now."

Her smile didn't fall, but it did change, growing more serious. When they were close, they stopped their descent. "We haven't come to go with you."

Orla cocked her head. "Then, why are you here?"

The man answered in a heavy brogue. "We traveled here from Ireland with a large group of half-fae and have come across many others making their way to the safety of Los Angeles. We came to tell you we don't know anything of your world, Prince. It does not belong to us."

The woman nodded. "We're staying here, in our own world. We won't give it up, not when we can create a haven for all those like us. The humans will learn to accept us in time.

You've given us the one thing we wanted. Hope." She laid a hand on Toby's shoulder. "And that is a priceless gift."

Toby bit back a grin as these half-fae restored part of his faith. The easy path would be to go to the fae realm, but they wouldn't betray themselves or their hearts.

Finally, Orla's lips lifted. "Welcome to L.A. This is your home now."

They were words Toby expected to say to the half-fae once they returned to Eldur, yet they felt right here in this realm.

As he watched them smile and laugh, he realized giving up his portal magic meant nothing compared to everything else he stood to lose.

Chapter Twenty-Seven
SOPHIE

Sophie slammed into the ground with a thud, the coarse dry grass of Eldur scratching her face. Toby's portals were much calmer, but she still hadn't mastered the landing.

"That was a spectacular fall." Gulliver stood over her with a smile, offering her a hand. She took it, and he pulled her up, his tail brushing the grass from her clothes.

Toby had sent them back to retrieve Noah, but Sophie didn't want to think about leaving. Not so soon after their arrival.

"I will never get used to that." She stared into his feline eyes, happy to see the real Gullie again.

"Oh." He snatched his tail away. "Sorry." He seemed to wilt before her eyes. "I forget it's a shock when we come back."

"What? No, Gullie." She laughed. "I meant the portal and the hard landing. And it was night five minutes ago, and now it's a beautiful afternoon." She pried his fingers off his tail and held it like she would his hand. She wasn't sure if that was done, but she needed him to know she wasn't ... afraid of his unique features.

His face flushed pink, and he smiled as they turned toward Aghadoon. She felt a little silly for holding his tail, but she really liked the smile it put on his face.

"You won't have to worry about portaling for too much longer." His tail snaked around her wrist and the soft leaf-like tip stroked the inside of her palm.

Sophie nodded. "It's for the best, don't you think?" She chanced a glance at him.

Gullie sighed. "For the safety of our people in the human realm, it is for the best. I'll just really miss ... tacos."

"Tacos? You're going to miss tacos?" Sophie laughed. It wasn't the first time he'd made the claim.

"It's really the best food in all the worlds." He patted his flat stomach.

"I'm sure we can come up with a fae equivalent."

"We can?" He tilted his head at her like he didn't understand the concept of recipes.

"Sophie! You're back!" Noah raced through the pillars of Aghadoon and slammed right into her. "I was afraid the humans wouldn't let you leave."

His shoulders trembled as he buried his face in her side and clutched her waist like he'd never let go.

"Hey." She wrapped her arms around his small frame and held him close. "Look at me, Noah."

He tilted his head back but refused to move.

"I promise you, I will never leave you on your own. You're my family now."

"I am?"

She leaned down to his level. "Guess what I found out?"

"What?" He blinked at her with his startling golden eyes.

"*Your* mother was *my* mother." She grinned. "She's not with us anymore, but I can tell you, she loved you so much."

"Truly?" Noah's eyes filled with tears. "I get to keep you?"

"Well, you're my brother, and I have always, always wanted a little brother." She brushed the wavy curls from his face. "And I couldn't be happier that I get to keep you." She hugged him close, her heart melting when his little arms wrapped around her neck. This kid ... he was everything.

"What about your dad? He doesn't like people like me." He dropped his arms and stared at the ground.

Sophie shared a look with Gulliver. This kid just broke her heart.

"That's why I had to leave." She took Noah's hand. "I had a few things to say to my dad."

"And?" Noah mumbled.

"And he won't be part of our lives anymore." She squeezed his hand to reassure him.

"Really?"

"Really." She smiled. "It's just you and me, Noah."

A hesitant smile lit his face. "Come on, I have to show you the magic library. It's so cool!" He tugged on her hand, and she had no choice but to follow him into Aghadoon. "It's so much better than the library at the institute. And there's another library at the palace, but it's not magic like this one. It shows you what you want to read. I still can't read, but Uncle Griff started teaching me."

"Uncle Griff?" Sophie laughed at his exuberance.

"Yeah, he said I could call him that. Is that okay?"

"Of course." Sophie and Gullie followed Noah down the newly repaired street to the library.

"Welcome back." Griffin met them on the porch. The library itself remained whole, but the village was still undergoing repairs, and fae were coming and going with tools and carts, working together to rebuild.

"I need to borrow Gullie for a little while. Will you two be comfortable alone in the library?" Griffin asked, a serious look on his face.

"What's wrong now?" Gullie sighed.

"Some of our visitors in the camp can't decide if they want to stay or go home to the humans. They want to talk to you."

"Me?" Gulliver glanced around like his father might be talking to someone else.

"Yes, you. They trust you. They want to know more about Myrkur. Some of them like the idea of staying here, but they can't decide if they want to stay in Eldur. I think they'd be more comfortable in Myrkur, where we don't have so much magic. Will you talk to them?"

Gulliver nodded, turning to Sophie. "Will you be okay here for a little while? I'll be back as soon as I can."

"Sure. I think we can entertain ourselves for a bit." Sophie glanced down at her brother with a smile. "You go on and do your thing."

"Okay. I won't be long." Gullie turned to leave with his father.

"Now, don't let Noah drive away with the village while we're gone," Griffin hollered over his shoulder.

The sound of Noah's laughter caught Sophie by surprise. She'd never heard him laugh before.

"Where's your favorite place in the village besides the library?" she asked.

"The square!" Noah grabbed her hand and hauled her off

the porch and down the street. "It's really pretty, and that's where all the magic stones are. Grandpa Brandon said he'd teach me how to align the stones once I learn to read."

"He did?" Sophie shook her head. It seemed while she was away, her little brother had been busy winning over some hearts.

They arrived at a small grassy square near the center of the village. "Let's sit in the sunshine for a bit while we wait on Gullie." Sophie sank down on the lush carpet of green grass, marveling at how vibrant it was under the unforgiving Eldur sun.

"This place is so magical, isn't it?" Noah said, as if answering her thoughts.

"And so pretty," she added, studying her brother's face. He looked healthier here. His cheeks were fuller, and the shadows under his eyes had vanished.

"The healers have been giving me potions."

"Can you still read my thoughts like before? I can't hear you."

Noah shrugged. "Not really. It's different here. Quieter. I still kind of know what you're thinking, but it's not the same. I like it. You should see if you can do it, Soph. Just sit back and let all your thoughts go for a minute and try to feel what I'm thinking."

Sophie took a deep breath and tried to release all the nagging thoughts and decisions constantly swirling in the back of her mind.

"You're not very good at this. Try closing your eyes."

Sophie smiled and did as her brother suggested. Tilting her head back, she let the sun warm her face, clearing her mind.

A moment later she opened her eyes and studied her brother again. "The potions are helping you get your strength back. And you've been spending most of your time outside in the fresh air and sunshine. Queen Alona has been feeding you well too."

"Good job, Sophie. You did it."

"I think that was more you than me, kiddo." She chuckled. "You're the one with the magic."

"But not here. At least, not like I had in the human realm." He shuddered, dropping his head down to stare at the grass.

"You'll get your magic back when we go home."

"You know, there's all different kinds of magic here," Noah said. "Some is like mine, but others are more subtle. Like Gullie's defensive magic and Grandpa Brandon's Gelsi magic. I don't know what a Gelsi is, but he has to use words to make his magic work. So, he doesn't lose control like I always do. He just has to speak the right words with the right intent and things happen exactly the way he wants them to."

"You like it here, don't you?" Sophie asked carefully.

"I love it. The people here are nice. It's like a big family, and they let anyone join. I've never had that before. And they don't make you stay inside when you want to be outside. They have the best food, and when you ask for ham, you get the real stuff. Not the fake kind from a can."

"It can be like that anywhere, Noah. Not just here. When we go home, we'll find a place we like. We can settle down in Los Angeles with the other half-fae, so you'll be around people just like you. You can go to school, and I'll make all your favorite foods. We can have real ham there too, you know? We can be together there. Always."

"But I'll have magic there." Noah dropped his gaze again.

"We'll find you a teacher who can help you learn to control it."

"What if I wanted to stay here where I don't have to have that kind of magic?" He looked up at her. "Would you leave me?"

"I promised I would never leave you, and I meant it. But I don't think we can stay here, Noah. I have no way of making a home for us here. In L.A., I can get a job to pay for things." Though, she had no idea if waitressing would even bring in enough money to support everything she was promising him.

Noah nodded.

"Anyone hungry?" Gulliver called from down the street. "I brought snacks."

"I already ate before you guys came back." Noah scrambled to his feet. "I'm going to go pack my things."

Sophie thought she saw tears in his eyes just before he ran away.

"I brought all the best snacks." Gulliver laid a blanket on the ground. "I thought we'd have a picnic," he spoke so fast, Sophie couldn't get a word in. "You'll love the pastries with the cream filling." He dumped out a pile of food on the blanket before he sat down. "They aren't the same as beignets, but they're close. And the meat pies here are excellent." He passed her a pie the size of her head. "A bit spicy like some of the New Orleans foods you like."

Sophie laid her pie down on the blanket. "I'm not really hungry." She took his hand. "There's a lot on my mind right now." She ducked her head, trying to meet his gaze, but he wouldn't look at her.

"Can't you stay for a few more days?" His voice cracked as he squeezed her hand, and his tail flicked sadly behind him. "Let's not say goodbye just yet."

"I have to do what's best for Noah," she whispered, her mind still reeling with decisions she couldn't seem to commit to.

"I'll never see you again." Gullie wiped his face, trying to mask his tears. "I'm not sure I'm ready for that."

"Oh, Gulliver O'Shea," she said his name like a prayer. "I think I have to stay here."

"What?" He finally met her eyes. "What do you mean? You want to stay in Eldur?"

"Noah likes it here. He's safer in this world. I just don't know if it's the right decision." She stood, pacing to the edge of the small village square to put some distance between them. She couldn't look into his beautiful eyes and make this decision for her little family.

"You want to stay for Noah." He said it like a statement. Like it was exactly what he'd thought she'd do in the end.

"No, you big dummy." She whirled around. "It's for me too." Now, she was the one who couldn't meet his gaze. "I just don't know if that means Eldur ... or somewhere else."

Gulliver closed the distance between them. "You can go wherever you want. I'll take you to all the kingdoms, so you can decide which you like best. It'll take longer since we won't be able to portal, but I don't mind."

"You're a good man," she whispered. "But you're a little slow when it comes to the ladies I think that's what I love most about you."

"Love?" He blinked at her, as if he still wasn't sure what she was trying to say. Maybe she was just as bad at this love stuff as he was. "I'll always look this way." He grabbed her arms, running his hands down from her shoulders to her wrists, letting his tail wind around them. "The Gullie you met in the human realm won't be here."

"The Gullie I met in the human realm was an odd sort of human. He isn't the one I fell in love with. The one who risked everything for me was this guy right here. Tail and all. And I think I'd like to stay with him."

"Yes!" Gulliver let out a whoop of joy as he hugged her tight. "I can't wait to show you Myrkur!" But his face fell.

"Only, I'm technically part of Tia's council, and she may make me move to Iskalt. It's really, really cold there. Did you hate it when you were there before?"

"Hush Gullie." She laughed. "We can figure all that out later. But would you kiss me already?"

"I can do that." He grinned and leaned in close to press his lips to hers, pulling her against his chest.

Sophie let her arms snake around his neck, her fingers trailing through his hair as his tail wrapped around her arm. She sighed into his kiss, thinking she was finally home.

"Aw! Loch, can you believe it?" The hiss of Brea's voice interrupted their moment. She sounded so much like her daughter. "Gullie got the girl!" She moved from her hiding spot around the corner, tugging her husband along behind her. "I'm so proud."

"I hope you know what you're getting into," Lochlan said.

"Er ... Happiness?" Gulliver hugged Sophie to his side, his face almost the same color as the Eldur sun.

"No. I was talking to Sophie." He shook his head. "As Tia's father and Gulliver's uncle, I will tell you that life will never be dull with these two around, and I'm afraid they come as a package deal."

Chapter Twenty-Eight
GULLIVER

Someone pounded on the library door, and just like they had for the last three days, Tia, Toby, and Gulliver ignored it.

"We're nearly ready, aren't we?" Gullie asked, peeking over Tia's shoulder at the crimson Gelsi scribbles he couldn't fully understand. Though, he could pick out enough words to get the gist of what it said.

"You can't rush magic, Gullie." Tia tried to wave him away. "Especially the kind we're doing here. Mom is going to murder me for letting you two talk me into this."

"Wait, are you sure about that word there?" He pointed to the Fargelsian word for destroy. "Should it be *springa*, or something more like *svero*. That means to cut, right? Or maybe *skera?*" But Gullie was pretty sure that was the word to sever a spell.

"Good catch, Gul." Toby scratched out the word on his copy. "It should probably be *svero*, don't you think, Tia?"

"*Eyoa*," Tia muttered, and *springa* vanished from the parchment she was working on. "He's actually right. It should be *svero*. How did I not catch that?"

"We're not exactly working under the most ideal circumstances." Toby gave her shoulder a squeeze.

"I still don't know if we're doing the right thing, Tobes. Are you sure this is going to work?"

"It has to." Gulliver paced across the library, once again wishing he could be more help to his friends with magic.

The knocking at the door grew more persistent.

"Are you three ever coming out?" Griffin shouted. "The humans are going to start getting violent again. They want a resolution, and they want it now."

"Should I tell him we need another hour?" Gulliver leaned against the rattling door to keep his father out.

"No." Tia's brow furrowed. "I think we're done. Now, we just have to see if it works." She rolled up the old parchment and tucked it into her pocket. "Time for you to go tell everyone." Tia nodded at Gulliver as she stood up from the chair she'd occupied for most of the last three days.

"Me? Why do I have to do it?"

"Because it was your hairbrained idea to begin with." She patted him on the back and steered him toward the door.

Gulliver was ready to bolt when they opened the door to an audience of impatient fae waiting in the moonlight. After three days in the library, Gullie had lost all track of time.

"Well?" Griffin demanded.

"You three better have a solution to this mess." Brea stood

with her arms folded across her chest, and Lochlan glared at them along with the other royals of the five kingdoms. They even dragged Kier away from covering Iskaltian duties for Tia.

The rest of the crowd just looked scared.

Gulliver saw so many familiar faces. Ones he loved like family and ones he'd only recently met from the human realm. Yet, they were all fae. And they all needed a solution that worked.

"So, we came up with—" he began.

"*You*. You came up with the idea," Tia corrected him.

"Okay, *I* had an idea that we should ask the library to show us the original O'Shea magic. The origin spell that gave the O'Sheas the ability to portal."

"And?" Griffin urged him to continue.

"And we found it." Gulliver kicked his boot against a loose board of the library porch.

"And what have you done with it?" Brea asked, but her gaze lingered on her daughter.

"Our first thought was to destroy it. Destroy the O'Shea legacy," Tia said. "The way you destroyed the marriage magic all those years ago."

"But we came up with a better idea," Gulliver said.

"*You*. You came up with this nonsense," Tia insisted.

"Fine. I suggested we—and by we, I mean Tia—edit the origin magic. It turns out the ancient O'Sheas and O'Rourkes were in this together. The spell was written in Fargelsian and enacted with Iskaltian magic."

"We redesigned the magic," Tia interjected. She pulled the scroll from her pocket.

"Is that written in blood?" Brandon's eyes widened in alarm.

"It is." She shied away from her grandfather's gaze.

"Tia, we don't mess with that kind of magic."

"Well, I didn't make it that way; our ancestors did. And it's our responsibility to fix what they broke." She lifted her chin in defiance.

"Whose blood is it?" Brea asked softly after the crowd fell silent.

"Mine and Toby's."

Gulliver felt bad for her. She sounded like ten-year-old Tia again. The one who'd worked with her mother to bring down the barrier around Myrkur that had made it a prison world for generations. That had been risky magic then, and they were about to take an even greater risk now. And it was all his idea.

"We're dealing with two separate realms," Gulliver spoke up. "To fix the tears in the veil caused by the O'Shea magic, it has to be healed from both sides."

"But why rewrite such dangerous magic?" Brea asked. "Couldn't we find another way to heal the veil? One that doesn't involve blood magic?"

"The only other way to fix this is to destroy the original spell." Brandon sighed. "And I don't even know if that will heal the veil. It will just make it so we can't destroy it further."

"That would be the safest approach," Griffin said.

"But it would be the end of O'Shea magic. The end of portaling."

"I think we can all agree that is something we can learn to live without," Lochlan said.

"But what if we didn't have to?" Tia raised her voice over the murmurs of the crowd. "Hear me out. Portaling has become a tool we all depend on. It facilitates travel between the kingdoms. It keeps us close. It melts away the distance separating the kingdoms and makes our jobs as leaders much easier."

"But we can travel the old-fashioned way," Brea insisted. "It takes longer and more effort, sure, but we will do everything in our power to keep the families of the five kingdoms close. We are family. We will endure."

"Right, *we* will." Tia nodded. "For this generation. And maybe a few more. But without portaling, we will naturally drift apart. Our families will divide and go their own ways, and in a few generations, we will be strangers again. And in a few more, potential enemies." Tia stepped down from the porch, her eyes earnest and pleading.

"All my life, I've watched you all work *so* hard to get where we are now. Growing up, we three have watched our parents do what is right. And we have helped you create the wonderful, flourishing world that the five kingdoms has become. Time and again, we have clawed our way out of a world divided by hate and cynicism.

"Our ancestors hated each other so much they created the vatlands to keep our kingdoms apart because they couldn't find a way to be at peace with each other. Right now, we can't see ourselves ever going back to that, but the truth of the matter is, it could happen all too easily."

"She's right." Gulliver stepped forward to join her. "We're friends now, but what happens in the future when we're nothing but strangers? What happens to my people who don't have magic of their own? Persecution at best? Another prison world at worst?"

"And what happens to Lenya if, in the future, we don't maintain the kind of relationships we have now?" Tia asked. "My husband is here to see to their wellbeing now, but they are completely reliant on us to give them the crystals they need for their own magic. How easily could that support be pulled?"

"You've made your point, my Queen." Lochlan nodded his approval. "Now, what is your solution?"

"We keep portaling, but we change the rules." Gulliver

pulled a piece of paper from his pocket, where he'd drawn the solution to all their problems.

"Right now, the O'Sheas have to travel across the veil to the human realm and back again to visit another kingdom." He pointed to the line down the center of the page that represented the veil. "So, we change the direction of the magic."

"Rather than destroy the magic completely," Tia continued, "we make it so the O'Sheas can travel from one kingdom to the next without the necessity of passing through the veil first."

"And on the other side," Gulliver pointed to the circle representing the human realm, "any O'Sheas there could do the same, traveling from one place to another without the need to pass through the veil first."

They were met with silence and wide-eyed stares.

"I tried to amend the origin magic to give the ability to more than just the O'Sheas," Tia said. "But we were locked into the blood magic of the original spell. O'Shea blood binds the spell, so we were able to amend the magic to give portaling to anyone with a significant blood relation to the O'Sheas, not just a direct descendent. That was the best we could do," Tia said with a shrug. "We thought it was a good fix."

After a few moments of silence, Griffin cleared his throat. "It is, Tia. It's an extraordinary fix."

She nodded. "All right. If we're going to do it, though, we need to do it now. Time is of the essence because the longer we wait, the angrier the human leaders become."

"There's just one thing." Toby spoke for the first time, moving to stand with his sister. "To activate the magic, it has to be done from both sides." He shared a look with Tia. "That is one of the reasons Tia opened the magic to include more O'Sheas. She was hoping there would be a close enough relative on the other side of the veil to enact the magic."

"It will work best if there's an O'Shea to do it, but just in case there isn't, I added an amendment to the spell so it can be enacted without magic—hopefully. Someone just needs to take a copy of the spell written in our blood and burn the edges of the page, and then immediately submerge it in water under the light of the moon. Using moonlight, fire, and water will cause the spell to engage, and the veil will be healed and sealed off from our world forever."

"But if we had an O'Shea volunteer, it would be that much better," Toby added softly, staring right at Xavier on the edge of the crowd. "With or without magic, a direct descendent would be ideal."

"What are you saying, Toby?" Tia's voice cracked as Toby stepped down from the porch.

"I'm saying, I'll be the one to set the spell in motion from the other side."

Chapter Twenty-Nine
TOBY

"What? No!" Tia rushed down the steps to gather around Toby with Brea and Lochlan.

"You can't be serious." Brea brushed shaking fingertips across his cheeks. "You know what it would mean?"

"I could never come back." Toby had known this was going to be hard, but he'd thought long about his decision, and it was the right one. For him. That didn't make it any easier to break his sister's heart.

"You don't have to be the one to make this sacrifice, son." Lochlan said, his eyes searching Toby's for answers. "No one does. At least, not yet. We can find someone on the other side to do this."

"Let's give Toby some space." Gulliver pulled Tia away. "I think your brother is trying to make a grand gesture." He nodded toward Xavier.

"Thanks, Gul." Toby was grateful his sister would have Gulliver when he was gone. She would need him now more than ever.

"What?" She gaped at Gulliver, tears in her eyes. "He can't do this, Gullie." She let him guide her toward her husband.

"What would you do if it was Keir on the other side?" He stared into her eyes. "You have to let him move on from Logan."

That was the thing about Gulliver O'Shea. He had more empathy than anyone Toby had ever known. Of course he was the one to get what Toby was trying to do. His sister was in good hands between Kier and Gullie. Knowing that was the only thing that had given him the strength to do what his heart wanted more than anything.

His heart broke as Tia buried her head against Keir's chest as though she could keep this from happening. Keir murmured something to sooth her, and she relaxed, but she couldn't seem to stop her tears.

"What are you doing?" Xavier asked as Toby closed the distance between them and reached for his hand. "This is your home."

"It is." Toby sighed. "And almost everyone I love is here. Except for the one person I don't think I can live without."

"We're in the middle of a war," Xavier protested, searching Toby's eyes for the truth of what lay between them.

"Perhaps. Maybe it will be over soon."

"We don't have magic like you have here."

"I don't have magic at all." Toby laughed. He turned to look at his parents and siblings, raising his voice. "Imagine living in a world where everyone around you has powerful magic and all you can do is open a door. Imagine for one second how that feels. To be born a prince without magic in this land makes you completely useless."

Brea started to protest, but Toby kept talking. "Normally, a royal born without magic would have been sent into the serving class when he came of age, but I was spared that fate.

"Now, I want you all to imagine what it was like for me to travel to the human realm to find others just like me. A whole community of fae with little or no magic. For the first time in my life, I felt useful. Their cause became my cause. I felt for these fae. I fought for them. And I fell in love with one of them." He took both of Xavier's hands in his.

"If they'll have me, I will continue to fight for them. I will use my portal magic to protect them. To facilitate the same level of communication and friendship that we have here. In the coming years, I hope to see more and more fae communities spring up across the globe. And I want to be there to see it happen.

"If Xavier will have me, I can be happy there. I can have a fulfilling life with someone I love at my side. I'm not sure I can or want to have that anywhere else with anyone else."

In a breath, Xavier rushed forward and pulled Toby into his arms with a bruising kiss, to the cheers of the half-fae still waiting to return home. That kiss held the promise of the kind of life Toby hadn't been sure was in his reach. After Logan died, his heart had shriveled up and died too. Xavier brought him back to life.

"I wasn't sure how I was going to leave you." Xavier pressed his forehead to Toby's. "I didn't want to, and I've tried so hard not to love you like I do, but it's impossible. If so many fae weren't counting on me back home, I would stay here with you, but I can't."

"That is why I'm coming with you." Toby held him close, careless of the people watching them.

"But are you sure you can leave your family behind?" Xavier searched his eyes. "I can't ask you to do that for me. I won't. I love you, but I don't ever want you to resent me for a rash decision."

"It's not rash." Toby shook his head. "Since Logan died, I've been searching for something—a life of my own without him, and I couldn't find it anywhere here. Not until I found you and your people. I've made my choice, and it's you and the world you are building for fae like us. I want to be part of it all."

Xavier nodded. "I'm in it, Toby. If this is what you want, I'll be with you every step of the way. I just want you to be sure."

"I've never been more certain about anything." Toby turned to his parents. "I don't want to leave you, Mom, Dad." His voice broke, and he was suddenly in Brea's arms as she sobbed.

"It's going to be okay, Mom." He held her tight, not wanting to let go, but knowing he had to.

"I know, son." Brea pulled away, staring into his eyes. "You make me so proud to be your mom." She brushed a hand over his brow like she did when he was just a boy. "I've watched you since Logan died and you haven't been yourself. No mother wants to see her son lose everything before he's had a chance to live."

Tears swam in Toby's eyes as she let him go.

"The farmhouse is yours now. Take whatever you need. Sell it if you want. All the documents you'll need are in the safe, along with enough human money to keep you afloat for a few months. There's also a substantial bank account. Xavier will know what to do with it." Brea gave him a last hug and stepped back, wiping her tears.

"If this is what you need to do, my son, you have our support." Lochlan wrapped his long arms around Toby. "I'm so proud of the man you've become. I wish you the best of everything in your new life. I'm just sad we won't be there to see it. But I want you to remember we are always right here with you." He placed a hand over Toby's heart. "Even if you can't see us, we're with you."

All he could do was nod at his father's final words to him, and then he was fumbling through his goodbyes with Griffin.

"I know we don't speak about it, but I am proud to be your father. Lochlan is your dad, and that's the way it should be, but every now and then, I see a bit of myself in you and your sister. You made a tough decision today, and I'm proud of you for standing up and reaching for the life you want. I want you to know it's been one of the greatest joys of my life to be Uncle Griff to you and your sister."

Toby sniffed back his tears and hugged his uncle. "Please tell Riona and the girls how much I love them and I'm sorry I couldn't say goodbye."

The other royals were all there to say goodbye in a blur of activity. Uncle Myles and Aunt Neeve both had words of wisdom and a last hug for him, along with a letter for Mrs. Merrick and the rest of Myles' human family they would never get to see again.

Alona and Finn wished him well and let him know Logan would have wanted him to move on with his life wherever he could find joy. Saying goodbye to the young princess he'd always thought of as a sister was a lot harder than he imagined. Darra had been just as lost as he was when Logan died.

"You're going to make a great queen someday, little Darra. Logan would be so proud of the young woman you've become."

"He loved you so much," she whispered against his shoulder. "I know he would want this for you."

He released her with a pang of regret for what might have been.

Toby had said all his goodbyes, except for the hardest one. He turned toward Tia, his emotions raging just under the surface.

"Tobes," Tia choked out his name, twisting her hands together. "You're the best part of me. How am I supposed to do this?"

"I don't know." His voice broke. "I'm so sorry, Tia." She rushed into his arms, and they held on to each other for dear life. "I don't know if I'll be able to amplify your magic once the veil is sealed."

Tia gave a snort at that. "Tobias O'Shea, I would give up every ounce of my magic to see you happy with someone you love."

"I just hope I'm doing the right thing." He sighed into her hair, her head tucked against his shoulder. "I know it's what I want. I worry some day you might need your amplifier and I won't be here, and then you'll be in harm's way because I once made a selfish decision."

"You hush." Tia pulled away from him, wiping the tears from her eyes. "You are the most unselfish fae any of the worlds have ever known. You deserve whatever happiness you can find, and I want you to go out there and take it and never be sorry."

"Thank you, Tia." He held on to her for a little longer before turning away. "I think I'm ready." There were so many others he needed to say goodbye to—people he would miss, but there was no time. The humans were growing impatient, and the outbreak of a full-blown war rested on his ability to leave his family behind and fix the damage he and his ancestors had made in the veil.

"You have everything you need?" Gulliver asked, his shoulders hunched.

"You know I'll miss you every bit as much as Tia?"

"Really?"

"Of course. You're like a brother to me too, you know." Toby couldn't believe after all these years that Gulliver didn't know that.

"You're making the right decision. I've been with you since this whole thing started. I've seen first-hand how their fight has become yours, and how Xavier has helped you move on from Logan. But I'll miss you. You're the one fae who can talk Tia down from her highs and lows. I don't know what I'm going to do without you."

"You'll manage." Toby smiled. "Am I wrong, or have you and Sophie made some big decisions too?"

Gulliver's ears turned pink as he glanced back to the human girl with the blue hair. "She's decided to stay. With me."

"Look at that, Gullie got the girl." Toby grinned and pulled Gulliver in for a last hug. "Take care of Tia for me. And I apologize in advance. I don't think you realize you're going to have to be you and me all rolled into one fae she won't be able to do without. But at least now, she has Kier."

The blood drained from Gullie's face as he nodded. "Don't worry about Tia. You know I'll be whatever she needs me to be."

"You're a good fae, Gul." Toby let him go. He couldn't stand anymore goodbyes. It was time. Time for him—the magicless fae—to fix the damage his ancestors caused.

"Before you go." Gulliver reached into his bag for something. "I don't know if this will work on the other side, but you should take it, just in case." He handed Toby a well-worn journal.

"You think?" He tucked it into his bag full of memories he couldn't do without.

"It's worth trying. I'll see that she checks hers in a few days, once you've had time to settle down."

"Are you sure absolutely about this, Toby?" Xavier stepped up beside him, his eyes full of questions.

"It's hard to leave them all." He glanced around the streets of Aghadoon, at his family. "I will miss them so much, but I've never been more sure about anything."

He took Xavier's hand, and together, they led their fae to the village square.

"Is everyone who wants to go home here?" Toby called across the crowd of half-fae. His family stood at the edge of the square, having said their goodbyes.

"We're all here," Orla said. "And eager to get back to L.A. and our new homes."

"Here, here!" someone in the crowd said.

"Oh! I forgot one thing." Toby searched the sea of faces, looking for his sister. "I need one last word with my queen before I leave."

Tia nodded and made her way through the throng of people. "I am here," she said, her face pale in the afternoon sunshine.

Toby moved to kneel before his sister. "My Queen, I would like to renounce my titles and my positions as Prince Tobias of Iskalt. I wish to enter my new life as just another fae."

Cool hands cupped his face and lifted his chin. "Prince Tobias O'Shea, the Ogre Killer, you could never be just another fae," she whispered. "But I will grant your request." Her voice lifted. "You will leave here as Tobias O'Shea, my brother and friend." She pulled him to his feet and flung her arms around him. "Now, go be happy." She choked and stepped back.

"I'm ready now." Toby gave a final wave to his family,

wishing for one moment he could have a last look at Iskalt before he said goodbye forever.

"Let's take our fae home." Xavier held his hand and they moved to the center of the square. "Just a quick question." He leaned in to whisper, "Why did your sister just call you the Ogre Killer?"

Toby snorted a laugh at that. "Long story."

"You'll have to tell me about it sometime."

"I really hope this works," Toby whispered, checking to make sure he had his copy of the O'Shea spell.

"It will. I have confidence in you and your sister." Xavier stepped back to let Toby open a portal big enough to take them all safely to L.A.

With a deep breath, Toby called on the only magic he had, hoping he would get to keep it, but if he had to give it up, he was happy to do that. It wouldn't make him any different from the other fae in his new home. And that was a prospect that made this difficult thing so much easier.

The magic filled him, rattling his bones with the intensity of it as it burst out of him. A crack of light slashed across the clearing where he stood. As he guided his portal magic, the crack widened into a swirling mass of light, widening to create a doorway large enough for all to pass through.

He could just make out the Hollywood sign near the park where Aghadoon had stood for a short time. The sun shone through the portal, contrasting with the darkness of the Eldurian night. Toby's heart kicked up a notch as he realized he couldn't wait to get back.

One by one, the half-fae who called the human world home made their way through the portal until only Xavier remained.

"I won't hold you to it if you decide to stay. You're giving up ... everything, and I don't want you to do it just for me."

"I'm doing it for us." Toby watched as Xavier stepped through the portal.

He held it open a minute longer, waving to his family one last time. He memorized their faces, making sure every detail was emblazoned in his mind.

"I love you!" he called to them and stepped through to the other side.

The silence was what caught Toby's attention first. Los Angeles was one of the loudest and busiest human cities he'd ever visited, even this late at night. He'd been counting on the chaos of the city to keep him distracted when the portal closed forever behind him.

"Why is it so quiet?" Xavier asked.

"The humans have mostly left," a fae Toby only vaguely remembered said. "Some remained, but they are friends. Our numbers are in the tens of thousands, and more arrive every day."

"So, it's truly our city now?" Orla asked, her eyes bright with hope.

"As long as the fae with magic follow through on their promises to seal the veil, then this is our home. Forever," the lady said.

"That's Meara," Xavier leaned in to remind Toby. "She's the leader of the Hollywood Hills fae."

"Thanks." Toby moved to the middle of the park. "Could someone bring me a basin of water?" He set his bag on the ground, fishing out the scroll written in his blood.

"This isn't your kingdom, Prince," Meara said. "No one will do your fetching for you."

"He isn't a prince anymore. He's one of us," Orla snapped. "And he needs water for the magic that will heal the veil and close it from this side. Someone get the man some water and a lighter."

"Will you need anything else, Toby?" Orla asked.

"No. Just fire and water. And someone to tell me what a lighter is," he added.

"It's like the magic sticks you use to light candles at home," Xavier explained, crouching down beside him in the darkness.

"This is home now." Toby smiled to himself as he laid the spell on the grass. Written with a mixture of his and Tia's blood, this was powerful magic, the likes of which no fae he knew had ever meddled with.

With the moon shining above, his Iskalt power came alive in a way it never did during the day. Though he didn't have much magic, he was still of Iskalt, and Tia believed that was enough to ignite the spell.

Fae gathered around to watch as Xavier helped Toby light the edges of the scroll, letting the flames curl and burn the parchment. Without a word, he dropped it into the basin Meara had brought him, and the flames flickered out. Blood seeped from the page, leaving the words behind in black lettering. Toby fished it out and laid it flat on the ground, waiting for something to happen.

"It didn't work," someone said.

"Give it a minute," another replied.

Heat shot through Toby's body, lighting him up from the inside.

"Toby!" Xavier shouted as Toby collapsed to the ground.

"I'm okay." He gasped. "Look!" He pointed to the sky where a rainbow of colors moved like the Southern Lights of the snúa aftur in Eldur. He and Logan used to sneak out to watch them in the summer. Colorful light streaked like threads of magic, healing the veil where it had been destroyed by the O'Shea magic.

"It's beautiful," Xavier whispered, staring up into the heavens.

"Magic is always beautiful. Big or small." Toby stood there holding Xavier's hand as the last of his sister's magic faded from the sky.

"Did it work?" Orla asked.

"Only one way to find out." Toby moved away from the crowd and tried to open a new portal. With thoughts of Iskalt filling his mind, he reached for his magic, but it wouldn't come. He couldn't feel his childhood home the way he always had before.

Shaking his head, he stopped trying. "It worked."

Sadness filled him as the finality of it all struck him hard. He could never go home. It was his choice, but it still hurt.

Cheers went up all across the park, and Toby wanted to celebrate with them, but a heaviness filled his heart.

"You okay?" Xavier asked.

"Yeah. It's just so ... final."

"You're allowed to be sad, Tobes."

"Thank you." He leaned into Xavier's side.

"You think you can still open portals just on this side?"

"Probably. I can still feel the O'Shea magic. It just won't let me reach across the veil."

"Give it a shot. I was thinking we could spend a night at a certain farmhouse. I think you've earned at least one quiet night before we jump into rebuilding our world together."

"I'll try." Toby reached for his magic and a familiar sensation filled his chest. The light of his magic glowed, and a swirling doorway opened to reveal the farmhouse that held wonderful memories of his family.

"There it is!" Xavier cheered. "See, Tobes, you still have a home here. It's not the end of the fae for you. It's a whole new world for us and all of our fae."

He stepped through the portal, and with a smile, Toby followed.

Chapter Thirty
SOPHIE

"This is a strange sort of contraption." Riona struggled with the yards of lacy fabric.

"It's called a veil." Sophie giggled as Riona tried to arrange the 'contraption' on her head.

"It's a silly *human* thing, isn't it?" Riona gave the veil a frightening scowl. Frightening if you didn't know the woman behind the scowl.

"It's a tradition." Sophie reached up to help her arrange the layers of pearly lace studded with silver and blue stars. "When I was sick, I used to dream of the wedding I'd never have, and I always wanted a long veil that would trail behind me."

"Well, you look beautiful."

"Thanks, Riona."

"Call me Mom." Riona busied herself with fussing over Sophie's dress, but Sophie knew the woman wasn't the sort to make grand emotional gestures. "That is, if you want." She stopped to meet Sophie's gaze in the mirror. "I don't want to take the place of your own mother. Especially today."

"I never really knew her. Not as an adult anyway." Sophie's eyes filled with tears. "And you've been like a mother to me since I met you. I'd love nothing more than to call you Mom."

"Well, don't cry." Riona wiped the tears from Sophie's cheeks. "We don't want to send you out there with puffy eyes." She smiled, moving to arrange Sophie's dress. A fairytale work of art worthy of a princess. The subtle blush fabric fell like a waterfall of silk from her waist to the floor, and the bodice sparkled with tiny stars of silver, blues, and pinks. A sheer cape of intricate flowers and vines fell from her shoulders to trail behind her, blending perfectly with the veil of her dreams. Silver brocade and iridescent pearls studded the front of her gown from neckline to hem. She couldn't have dreamed of a more perfect dress for such a special day.

"Thank you for this," Riona said softly.

"For what?" Sophie turned to face her soon-to-be mother-in-law.

"For having the wedding here in Myrkur, where Gulliver has so many memories. It's your day, and I would have thought you'd want to have the wedding in Iskalt since it's your home now."

"My home is with Gulliver, and this is where he's from, where all his family is. I couldn't imagine having *our* special day anywhere else."

"The girls are so excited to be included. I just hope they behave themselves. I apologize in advance if they don't. You know they're a bit of a handful."

Niamh and Nora were Gulliver's eight- and ten-year-old sisters, who would be Sophie's flower girls today—another human tradition Sophie wanted to keep.

"I'm thrilled to have them stand with us today."

Gulliver's family had embraced Sophie and Noah from the moment they met, especially his little sisters. Noah and the girls had grown close over the last year, and the three were inseparable whenever they visited, and inconsolable when they had to be apart.

Sophie had heard a lot of comparisons between them and Tia, Toby, and Gullie as kids. She just hoped it would never fall to this little trio to save the world together.

"I think I'm ready," Sophie said breathlessly. She'd heard of brides having cold feet before their big day, but Sophie couldn't wait to march down that aisle and marry her best friend in all the worlds. Gulliver O'Shea was the best man she knew, and she couldn't believe she would be able to call him her husband within the hour.

"Not quite." Riona turned to retrieve a navy silk bag from the table. "Brea gave me some tips on human weddings." She reached in. "This is your something borrowed from Brea and Tia." She held up a pair of beautiful pearl earrings that matched her dress perfectly. "They each wore these at their own weddings."

Sophie was overcome that they would think of her human traditions.

"They're beautiful." She couldn't wait to thank them.

"Something new from Neeve." Riona pulled a silver bangle bracelet from her bag. "She wanted to give you something simple and elegant." She slipped the bracelet over Sophie's hand.

"It's engraved." Sophie read the inscription. "Love always finds a way. Gulliver and Sophie O'Shevereaux." She glanced up at Riona. "I thought he was joking about sharing our names?"

"He wants to take your name the way the humans do. And he wants you all to have a fresh start. You, Noah, and Gulliver are forming a little family of your own. I think it's fitting. You have a bittersweet past with your Devereaux family and Gullie had a difficult childhood before Griffin found him. And poor Noah never had a name of his own. Found families are extra special, Sophie. You three got to choose each other."

"I love it." Sophie clutched the bracelet to her heart. "Sophie-Ann O'Shevereaux." She tried out the name. "Has a nice ring to it, doesn't it?"

"It does." Riona took her hand in hers. "The something old is my gift to you." She pulled something from her bag. "It isn't much. I grew up in Myrkur when it was a prison realm, and the only things people valued were food and shelter. But this belonged to my mother, and I had it made into a hair pin for you."

It was very old. And Sophie recognized it immediately from the stories Gulliver had told her about his ferocious mother.

"It's your family crest." She shook her head. "I can't take this, Riona. It should be my something borrowed, and Brea's earrings can be my something old-slash-borrowed."

The pewter oiche blossom represented the sacred duty of Riona's family. Sophie didn't know much about that duty, other than the story of how Riona came to name the rightful ruler of Myrkur after the fall of King Eagan.

"No. I want it this way." Riona took the pin and clipped it into Sophie's hair. It blended perfectly with her veil.

"This should go to Niamh when she's older. She will likely inherit your legacy as your eldest daughter."

Riona smiled. "The sigil doesn't carry the legacy. Besides, you're my eldest daughter now."

Sophie pulled Riona in for a hug. "Thank you, Mom." She held her tight.

"Oh, I don't want to crush your veil." She pulled back. "I think we're done with the traditions, aren't we?"

"Something blue," Sophie said and both women started to giggle. "I forgot I dyed my hair with shadow berries."

"It's lovely." Riona tucked a strand of Sophie's long, vivid blue hair behind her ear. "And a perfect something blue."

"Gullie always seemed to like the blue hair, so I wanted to surprise him with it."

"You've been starting all kinds of new trends with the Myrkurian girls."

"Have I?"

"Oh, yes. I saw a girl in town the other day with blue tipped hair just like yours when you first arrived. And I imagine your beautiful human wedding will start all sorts of new traditions among fae brides. All the Myrkurian girls are fascinated with you, you know?"

"Me? Why?"

"Because you got Gulliver's attention. My son is many things, but a master with the ladies, he is not. Every girl in Myrkur has had eyes for him ever since he finally grew into his height, but he's never given them any notice. I think he was waiting for you."

"No wonder he moved so slow." Sophie shook her head and laughed.

"Are you nervous?" Riona went to fetch Sophie's bouquet of Ilmur flowers.

"Not at all. I'm excited." Sophie fidgeted in her dress, eager to get on with it.

"The last finishing touch." She handed her a bouquet of the

most beautiful white blossoms Sophie had ever seen. The flowers in Myrkur were rather dark with muted colors. These flowers came from Fargelsi, and they smelled wonderful. Sophie held them up to her face to inhale the heady scent.

"Oh, don't do that." Riona pulled her back just in time. "The scent is intoxicating up close. You'll be walking down the aisle like a magic-wielding fae after too much Gelsi wine. Or Gullie after a few sips of any wine."

"Oh." Sophie held them far out in front of her.

"The scent won't affect you unless you stuff your face into your bouquet."

"Got it." Sophie beamed at her future mother-in-law and did a little dance. "I'm so excited."

"Oh, dear." She whisked the flowers from Sophie's hands. "You are human." Riona studied her face. "Ilmur blossoms might not have been the best choice. You may need a break from the flowers from time to time. Just let me know if you start feeling funny."

"Okay." Sophie giggled, feeling as though she could walk on air.

Riona laughed. "This should be a fun evening. The gardens are full of Ilmur flowers Neeve sent over for the wedding."

"Take me to my husband!" Sophie's voice rang out as Riona took her arm to escort her to the garden, where she was about to marry the best man she knew.

Someone replaced Sophie's bouquet with a lovely bundle of shadow berry blossoms, and her head cleared some, though she still felt as though she was walking on air down the aisle. Tiny flowers bloomed as she walked over the grassy lawn, all her favorite fae seated on either side of the aisle. Eleven-year-old Noah walked beside her, looking handsome in his formal fae tunic that complemented her dress.

Niamh and Nora fluttered along before them, dropping pale blue flower petals. Their wings stirred the breeze of the mild Myrkurian summer. The gardens were breathtaking, but Sophie only had eyes for the tall young man who waited for her at the end of the aisle.

Gulliver stood nervously, his tail swishing behind him until he caught sight of her. All the nerves seemed to vanish as he darted down the aisle to meet her. Laughter swept through the crowd, and Sophie heard several whispers of, "Aw."

He seemed to realize at the last moment that he should have waited on her, but she grabbed his arm and the three of them took the final steps up to the front of the garden, where the King of Myrkur waited to perform the ceremony.

The heady scent of Ilmur flowers filled the air, but Sophie's mind was clear. Taking Gulliver's hand in hers, they approached the king, but they couldn't take their eyes off each other.

They'd come a long way from that first day when Gulliver wandered into the Vieux Carré Cafe. The scent of fresh beignets had lured him in and changed her life forever. She shuddered to think of where she might have ended up if it weren't for Gulliver.

She would have been with her mother and grandmother now, resting in the family mausoleum in the cemetery she'd visited often as a child. Instead, she was getting the fairytale happily ever after she'd only allowed herself to dream of. And it came with an incredible family who loved her as one of their own.

The ceremony passed in a blur as memories flooded Sophie's mind—happy and sad ones. Part of her missed her father today, but looking at Noah beaming up at her from his place between Niamh and Nora, she knew she was home.

"I love you, Soph," Gulliver whispered as his lips brushed hers and Hector announced them as Mr. and Mrs. O'Shevereaux.

Epilogue
FIVE YEARS LATER

Gulliver stepped through the familiar portal, leaving Iskalt behind, eager to see his wife after three days without her. Sophie was his world, but sometimes work got in their way. And for them, work always meant Tia. Gulliver still served as one of Tia's most trusted advisors, but so did Sophie.

She spent a great deal of her time with Tia, teaching her all things human so when she wrote to her brother, she would have a better understanding of his life in the human world.

And that meant Sophie went wherever Tia went because Tia was never far from her journal that served as her lifeline to Toby.

"There he is!" Sophie's voice reached him the moment he entered Fargelsi, with Griffin following right behind.

"Missed you, Soph!" Gulliver called, not caring who heard, no matter the teasing he got from the other royals. He loved his wife and didn't bother trying to hide it.

"Papa!" A gangly little boy with a tail ran across the garden, and Gulliver swept him up in his arms. "Missed you too, Fergus." He held him tight, smothering him with kisses until he shrieked with laughter.

"The festival is about to start." Sophie took his arm, and they walked down the hill to the palace gardens. It was time for the annual festival of lights—an event he looked forward to every year since he was a child.

"Where is Noah?" Gulliver scanned the crowds of children playing on the hillside.

"He's with the girls, as usual." Sophie pointed to a group of older children already dancing under the setting sun. Noah, almost sixteen now, danced with Niamh and Nora, their wings forming a cage around him to keep the other girls at bay.

"Sophie!" Tia came rushing up the lawn, clutching her skirts high. "I just got a message from Toby!" She blew the hair from her face. "Can you explain what a surrogate mother is?"

"Oh my." Sophie reached for the journal. "May I?"

Tia nodded, handing over the book she never let out of her sight.

"Oh, Tia! This is good news!" Sophie beamed. "You're going to be an aunt."

"We're going to be aunts?" She peered over Sophie's shoulder. "Where does it say that?"

Toby and Xavier had adopted a little fae girl a few years ago, but they wanted more children. It was difficult for the fae of the human realm to adopt. It wasn't yet legal for them to adopt human children, so they had mentioned trying other means.

"They've found a young fae woman to act as a surrogate for them. They just found out she's pregnant with Toby's twins. A boy and a girl."

"What? Wait? How? I'm so confused." Tia wore a scandalous look on her face. "Did my brother ... cheat on his husband with this girl?"

"No. Um." Sophie's cheeks went pink as she leaned over to whisper the details to Tia.

"Oh!" Tia leaned back. "Human magic really is remarkable! And a little bit gross." She shuddered. "But I guess that means Toby's twins will be O'Sheas?"

"Can someone explain what's happening, please?" Gulliver leaned in closer to make himself part of the conversation. "I'm going to be an uncle again?"

"Yes. They're Toby's biological children," Sophie explained. "They'll inherit the O'Shea magic."

"What does that mean?" Gulliver asked.

"Toby's legacy will live on in the human realm, and Tia's will live on here through Madison and Duncan." Tia's and Keir's four-year-old twins were miniature versions of Toby and Tia, and the apple of Iskalt's eye

"I just hope our kids are better at portaling than me." Tia beamed and rushed off to tell her parents the news.

"What worries will you send off into the sky tonight, Pappa?" Fergus asked from his spot on Gulliver's shoulder. Gus' tail wound around Gulliver's, and his son's cat-like eyes filled with adoration.

Gulliver took Sophie's hand, and they headed toward the gathering crowd as evening settled over the Gelsi palace. "I'm not sure, son," Gulliver said. "I don't really have any worries this year. Maybe I'll write down a few hopes for the future of the fae."

A new cowritten series by Melissa and M. Lynn begins soon! Sign up to get updates here!
https://bit.ly/Fantasy-SignUp

Thank You!

Thanks for reading Queens of the Fae!!
Want more by M. Lynn? Don't forget to check out her Six Kingdoms series.

Want more by Melissa A. Craven?
Find the Ascension of the Nine Realms series wherever you buy books

About Melissa

Melissa A. Craven is an Amazon best-selling author of Young Adult Contemporary Fiction and YA Fantasy (her Contemporary fans will know her as Ann Maree Craven). Her books focus on strong female protagonists who aren't always perfect, but they find their inner strength along the way. Melissa's novels appeal to audiences of all ages and fans of almost any genre. She believes in stories that make you think and she loves playing with foreshadowing, leaving clues and hints for the careful reader.

Melissa draws inspiration from her background in architecture and interior design to help her with the small details in world building and scene settings. (Her degree in fine art also comes in handy.) She is a diehard introvert with a wicked sense of humor and a tendency for hermit-like behavior. (Seriously, she gets cranky if she has to put on anything other than yoga pants and t-shirts!)

Melissa enjoys gardening and sitting on her porch when the weather is nice with her two dogs, Fynlee and Nahla, reading from her massive TBR pile and dreaming up new stories.

Visit Melissa at Melissaacraven.com for more information about her newest series and discover exclusive content.

Want to see more books by Melissa A. Craven? You can view them here

Join Melissa and Michelle's Facebook Group: Fantasy Book Warriors

About Michelle

Michelle MacQueen is a USA Today bestselling author of love. Yes, love. Whether it be YA romance, NA romance, or fantasy romance (Under M. Lynn), she loves to make readers swoon.

The great loves of her life to this point are two tiny blond creatures who call her "aunt" and proclaim her books to be "boring books" for their lack of pictures. Yet, somehow, she still manages to love them more than chocolate.

When she's not sharing her inexhaustible wisdom with her niece and nephew, Michelle is usually lounging in her ridiculously large bean bag chair creating worlds and characters that remind her to smile every day - even when a feisty five-year-old is telling her just how much she doesn't know.

See more from M. Lynn and sign up to receive updates and deals!

michellelynnauthor.com

Join Melissa and Michelle's Facebook Group: Fantasy Book Warriors

Follow Michelle and Melissa on TikTok

@ATaleOfTwoAuthors

Want to see more books by Michelle?

visit https://books2read.com/ap/R5my46/M-Lynn

www.ingramcontent.com/pod-product-compliance
Lightning Source LLC
Chambersburg PA
CBHW030529310726
48979CB00010B/1850/J
* 9 7 8 1 9 7 0 0 5 2 9 6 1 *